BEAUTY IS A BLADE

JUSTIN BOURNE BORING

LDP

Literary Dreams
PUBLISHING

Making literary dreams come true

LITERARY DREAMS PUBLISHING

Contents

Chapter 1
Mina Means Business

Y ou're goddamn right I mean business. I'm over two hundred years old, so my days of enduring narcissistic, lying, cheating assholes are over. Did I overreact by destroying an entire township in Jersey? Maybe, but sometimes you have to weigh consequences against comeuppance and scorch some earth. Sue me. I occasionally get a little stormy when someone rubs me the wrong way, but cheat on me, and you're gonna catch my claws. Fortunately for others, that didn't happen often. My heart wasn't as black as my long, straight hair or as pale as my alabaster skin, but I could be hard and unforgiving like my maternally inherited hazel eyes when it came to infidelity. I'm working on it.

Naturally, my shenanigans meant *they* would be coming for me, but it's okay; the just desserts were worth the calories. Besides, I'm finally ready to face *them*; it was long past due anyway- but that's a story for a little later.

I'm not the least bit ashamed to say I was deeply in love with a miserable phony prick for four years (a blink of an eye for me) or that I had recently agreed to marry said miserable phony prick a few days ago. When people are profoundly disingenuous about who they are,

one can't be blamed for trusting them. I wear my heart on my sleeve;
being powerful and ageless allows me to be vulnerable in ways others
can not. However, the downside is that you tend to go to extremes
when someone fucks you over.

Morristown, New Jersey? Collateral damage. Honestly, it was
worth it. There's little left in the world that commands my full and
total rage, and unfaithfulness is one of them. Not to mention, in all my
years, I've known only one thing sweeter than love, and that's revenge.

When I got the call from Auri, my bestie of over a hundred years, and
heard the frantic tone in her voice, I knew the shit was going down.

I answered my phone cheerfully, "Hello?"

"Mina? Hey, it's Auri," she blurted out.

"Hey, Auri. What's up? You sound...flustered." I wasn't used to
hearing my normally even tempered best friend so anxious.

"Flustered? Oh no, I'm pretty fucking far from flustered."

"What is it, girl? Are you okay?"

"I'm across the street from that little dive bar here in Morristown,
Goombas, and I'm staring at Roland...with his tongue crammed down
some bimbo's throat." She practically screamed through the phone.

I became solemn and quiet, "You're serious?"

"I'm serious, Mina. Here..."

In an instant, my text message alert chimed. I opened it up, and
there was a pic of Roland, my fiancé, my first true love in over 80 years,
with his plump, pink yazzick lapping some sluts cocksucker.

"Auri?"

"Yeah?"

"Get out of there right now." My voice went deadly calm.

"Wha-" Auri scarcely had time to react.

"Get. Out. Of. There. *NOW*!" I screamed.

"Okay, okay. But Mina, don't do anything rash -"

I hung up the phone and licked my drying lips. Motherfucker. Looks like Honeybear is going to have to rain down some sulfur.

I flung open my front door and strolled out onto the sidewalk in nothing more than a sheer blouse and skirt. All six feet six inches of me (significantly short by Pentavi standards) was vibrating with angry anticipation. I breathed in the fragrant spring air, but it did little to quiet my wrath. Goombas was only about a mile away, and it was a beautiful night, so I decided to walk there. Maybe it would give me a chance to cool down a bit. Maybe not.

As I sauntered down the street with my curvy, muscular hips stepping in time, I began heating up instead of cooling down. My eyes began to smolder, and my body temperature rose dramatically. I used my well-toned, She-Hulk-sized frame to rudely shoulder through a group of people hanging out and talking on the sidewalk. They began to shout and protest until they saw my burning eyes and felt the heat radiating off my body; then, they quickly backed away and took off like I was radioactive.

I left scorched footprints on the sidewalk with every bare step I took as the clothes I was wearing burned away from my body. The asphalt road next to me began to ripple and run like a black river as my hot, angry fury intensified. Cars driving past hit the asphalt pool and became stuck like dinosaurs in a tar pit, their wheels spinning before finally popping. The exterior paint on their cars began bubbling, the heat threatening to cook the people inside alive. Trees all around me suddenly burst into flame, while the buildings began to glow red hot. The windows started melting, and the bricks started exploding.

Pretty soon, the landscape behind me was a roaring fire about two thousand feet wide and growing. People were running and screaming from my epicenter as I strolled down the street like a violent act of nature. Buildings caught in my growing orbit began to wilt and run like warm butter. Cars were exploding and propelling embers into the sky that resembled a thousand devils' eyes as they rained down. This was only a small atom of my power.

As I approached Goombas, I saw Roland and his whore a few hundred feet down the road, fleeing the flames. He caught sight of me for a moment, and a terrible realization washed over him. They both made a mad dash towards a large church down the road while I slowly followed.

They began to stumble and waver within the field of my intense, inescapable heat. Finally, they fell to their knees and crawled toward the church doors in vain. They were on the verge of passing out, but Roland had the audacity to look pleadingly at me with those lying eyes.

That tore it. I unleashed every ounce of my power and focused it directly on them. Without warning, a fireball the size of an extinction level asteroid suddenly shot straight towards them, leaving a mile wide molten trench in its wake.

The two of them, dumbstruck, gawked in amazement as the white-hot comet instantly incinerated them, along with the church and a three-mile radius of Morristown, New Jersey.

The finale was an explosion the size of a small nuclear warhead that pushed a yellow and orange mushroom cloud towards the sky like a massive tombstone.

I thought of a fitting epitaph, "Here lies Roland. Roland lies, so Roland dies." I snickered and began to calm down a bit. I took a look around and marveled at the refreshing destruction. Hell hath no fury indeed. I continued to look around and noticed I was stark naked. "Damn, I need a Macy's."

I could hear all manner of sirens and helicopters converging on the area, so I ducked away swiftly into the swirling smoke and falling ash.

CHAPTER 2
THE STORY FOR A LITTLE LATER

As you have hopefully surmised by now, my name is Mina - no last name - just Mina. I live—sorry, *lived*, in skanky suburban Morristown, New Jersey, for the better part of 20 years. After two hundred and thirty-ish years, you would think I'd be a billionaire living in a cliffside mansion somewhere on the coast of Italy; or perhaps some kind of highfalutin CEO in control of a major corporation, but nope, I'm just Mina—Mina, formerly from the township formerly known as Morristown.

In any case, it has not been in my best interest to be high profile in the past, no matter the circumstances, but I was looking to make a change. Come out. My...*indiscretion* from the other night was going to draw some *consequences*, but I anticipated that. In fact, I took my ex-fiancé's infidelity as a sign that it was finally time for me to face my *eccentric* family ancestry and their clans. I had recently grown curiously restless with the thought of confronting them. I was unbelievably tired of hiding, and I felt pretty certain my power had reached its apex, so I was spoiling for a fight something awful. I couldn't explain the feeling inside my guts, telling me I could finally take them on, but it was irresistible. Roland got what he deserved for sure, but it was also a test run of my power, and I was convinced I was ready, ready for retribution.

I was Yasmani Ro, which meant I was the hated, mongrel bitch daughter of outlaw lovers from two ancient warring clans known as the Pentavi, an all-female shape-shifting clan, and the Sinteverete, an all-male warlock clan.

Being the only despised Yasmani Ro in the last hundreds of thousands of years meant both clans had been tenaciously looking to exterminate me—as they had my parents—since the day I was born.

A little backstory is in order. Thousands of years before the first organism crawled out of the primordial soup, the Pentavi and Sinteverete lived peacefully together as one; they were the Zol. The Earth realm was theirs until fire rained down from the heaven's, bringing new life with it. The destruction from their arrival and the evolution of this new life threatened the Zol and forced them into a vast, mystical realm, which they called Val Tebrae, accessible only through the conjuring of portals.

The Pentavi and Sinteverete lived together in Val Tebrae, angry and jealous of life in the Earth realm, which they perceived as having been taken from them. Their hatred of life on Earth grew and festered, poisoning their minds until mutual hatred was all they had. Naturally, it wasn't enough to keep them from eventually turning on each other.

The fuse was lit after a very talented, brilliant young Sinteverete warlock was instructed by the Elders to create a spell for agelessness called The Eonian. The Eonian, when cast by a Pentavi or Sinteverete clan member, allowed them to live forever and choose their age at will, but the spell was not synonymous with immortality. Members of the Pentavie and Sinteverete under the influence of The Eonian could still be killed, but only in battle. This provision, forced by the Elders, appealed to the Pentavi and Sinteverete Elder's burgeoning lust for war and power.

The toxic spell further exacerbated a gender divide between the clans and would soon lead to their uncoupling. Once the Pentavi and Sinteverete no longer needed one another to perpetuate the bloodlines, the chasm widened between the males and females.

The Pentavi and Sinteverete stopped training with one another, weakening their abilities and ensuring no one gender would ever be able to wield both clans' powers. Disputes degenerated into bloodletting, petty squabbles became war, and greed became God.

The Pentavi and Sinteverete people could no longer live together under one clan, so they split based on gender, known as the Great Divide, and criminalized having any more Yasmani Ro children. They no longer had to share anything with each other or future generations, so the clan Elders wanted everything for themselves. At the provocation of the Elders, the clans fought with one another for millions of years until a tense treaty was drafted. Both clans created laws in order to maintain the benefits, as well as their segregation. They were now forever in pursuit of domination over one another, the Earth, and all the other realms.

There were miles of rules and regulations behind this treaty between the Pentavi and Sinteverete clans, but it was their laws surrounding coupling and procreation that were the most binding. It was forbidden and punishable by the pain of torture and death for members of the Pentavi and Sinteverete clans to bear any more Yasmani Ro children.

The Pentavi and Sinteverete clan, along with their Elders, were all under the Eonian, like myself (thanks to my parents), but they possessed vastly different abilities. The Pentavi, for example, have superhuman strength and intelligence, are able to cast mid-level spells and can shape-shift into huge, regal feline creatures resembling jaguars, called yaggowar. The Sinteverete are powerful warlocks who can cast extremely high-level spells, have incredible strength and physical abilities, and are hyper-intelligent. Since I was trained by my parents in the ways of both the Pentavi and Sinteverete, I possess all their abilities. I never stopped training and doggedly honed every one of my skills. This gave me an incredible advantage over either side.

CHAPTER 3
A SLIGHT ALTERCATION

My parents met when war broke out on the Pentavi lands before moving to the blood-soaked battlefield of a war realm known as Reclon. There were hundreds of these war realms, but Reclon was the worst. It was lousy with monstrous beasts, some so big they could be mistaken for mountains. Massive tornadoes of toxic ash and acidic vapor swirled constantly, while oily black rain poured down, but those were the good days. When the seven suns came out, blood turned to vapor the moment it hit the air, and the heat could cook you like a sausage if you didn't constantly manage your protection spells. Savage tribes of mindless rouges fed off the coagulated blood and fetid flesh of fallen warriors, while vicious, poisonous, carnivorous plants constantly lay in wait for any and all unsuspecting victims. Caustic oceans and acid rivers cut through the jagged, rocky terrain like toxic arteries; it was a Hellscape of unimaginable cruelty.

My mother, Layluna, was once the highest-ranking General of the Pentavi warrior women. They were beautiful, elegant, and raw; she used to tell me when we were training. They were pale-white sisters of mine by blood, but they would want my heart in their hands. She couldn't stress enough how vitally important it was that I learn every molecule of knowledge surrounding the Pentavi *and* Sinteverete clans because they were both unshakably trying to kill me. It was a Hell of a way to grow up.

My mother seemed to cherish the time she spent with the Pentavi, reflecting proudly on her training and service to the clan. She was very young when the Great Divide split the genders but grew up and chose to remain at an adult age indefinitely, as most did. She largely supported their departure from the Zol and condemned the Sinteverete for their relentless pursuit of control over the Pentavi women. In the end, she would ultimately realize the Pentavi Elders were no better than the Sinteverete Elders in their selfish quest for power.

She was porcelain skinned like all Pentavi women and Sinteverete men, with a head full of long, abyss-black hair and a pair of deep green, emerald eyes like my own. She was a bold, brilliant, free-thinking spirit-of-fire, and I loved her dearly. Layluna always wore the traditional Pentavi Ceridome wraps until she passed them down to me. The Ceridome wraps were long, black silk strips decorated with elegant blood-red symbols and edged raggedly in gold to mark her rank. Almost like a mummy, the wraps crisscrossed chaotically over much of her body, except her head, hands and feet. The wraps were enchanted as well and accommodated yaggowar transformations with style and flair. Additionally, the straps would sheath and carry their weapons after yaggowar transformations. Being touched by magic, they were as hard as light armor but as flexible and breathable as cotton. Each Pentavi woman enchanted their wraps with different spells, making them a lethal weapon when needed. Equally as important, they carried the wearer's life story, usually one of warning. This was the uniform of the Pentavi and was embellished or decorated per the style and desire of the woman wearing them. Layluna was considered a bit of a rebel because she never wore armor, only her Ceridome wraps—nothing else.

She never wore anything within her long, flowing, midnight-black hair either, but she sometimes wore a large, round, black, flat amiboshi hat when there was bad weather. I, too, wear her Ceridome wraps, but far more discreetly; I wasn't trying to advertise it after all.

My father, Vasser the Voracious, was head of the Nevuscar, or The Undying, a very small, very formidable sect of seven Sinteverete warriors who are almost as old as the Elders. They are the most powerful Sinteverete warriors after the Elders and are truly immortal. While they cannot be killed traditionally or in battle, they are susceptible to incarceration and certain magic.

They possess a hyper-healing ability with one catch—they can only heal through the formation of scar tissue, so they do not generally retain their stunning good looks. When you see a Nevuscar, you know it.

My father, however, was impossibly handsome, possessed a classy, gentlemanly disposition and was very stoic. He was naturally pale and ghostly like the rest of us but was stippled with small gray freckles that made him very unique. He always wore his Absence of Light cloak, a cloak so black it was like staring into the Devil's heart. It was as powerful as a black hole, and fit like a tight coat, buttoned up the front by three rows of two side-by-side silver metallic coins. The massive hood enveloped his head and shoulders like a death shroud; only his two blood-red eyes could be seen floating within its lurking shadows. Always by his side was Sepultura, his cursed Blade of Black, one of the most powerful blades in all the realms. It had more trapped souls within its steel than any other of its kind.

The most important difference between Vasser and the other six Nevuscar was related to their rank and the reason Vasser was the lead; he had only one six-inch-scar that curved from the right corner of his mouth to the crux of his eye. Only my mother knew how he got the scar, but she never told me. Each of the other six Nevuscar knew their rank because they knew exactly how many scars they had, ranging from a couple hundred—Bael, Vasser's second in command—to several hundred thousand—Vasser's last in command, the Wrecking Ball. Any Nevuscar could tell you the story behind each and every one of their scars.

My father was a very rare breed. He was once married to a Pentavi woman before the Great Divide, but she was killed in the ensuing war. The Elders had long ago bred him to become a Nevuscar, which was only possible using special magic on an unborn Yasmani Ro child. He always fulfilled his obligations to the Sinteverete Elders but was a wild card. After the Great Divide, there were no more Yasmani Ro children; therefore, there were no more Nevuscar. Let me start from the beginning; I'll tell you how things came to be.

The shaky truce between the Pentavi and Sinteverete was quick to fall apart in the presence of any perceived slight from either side. The longest stretch of tense peace lasted for over fifteen thousand years - a blink of an eye to us—until one fine fall day in Val Tebrae, roughly four hundred years ago...

Maysiff, a fierce Pentavi warrior priestess, was hunting wild bock in the neutral territory of Rosh Simbique when a rare, very large, 62-point male bock emerged from the dense, brightly colored fall foliage about three hundred yards in front of her. He would be a real prize. She held her breath and soundlessly hunkered down on all fours. She exhaled her Alma, or soul smoke, and transformed into a yaggowar.

Though she was about eleven feet tall and twenty feet long, tail tip to nose, she was still smaller than the massive bock grazing before her.

Bock's are very similar to deer, but they are huge with an attitude exceeded only by their strength. Their massive antlers can inflict terrible, life-threatening wounds, and since taking one down was essentially a battle, it could kill her. That was the thrill of it all, though, wasn't it?

Maysiff crept closer and closer to the bock, choosing every step stealthily. The twin suns were at her back, blinding the prey to her presence, while her fiery orange and ashy black stripping pattern camouflaged her amidst the brightly colored leaves and background. She could hear all the sounds of the forest with focused clarity; She could see everything in brilliant definition with her large, gray cat eyes; and she could smell...everything. She could smell a dirty, disgusting Sinteverete sorcerer from a few miles away.

Maysiff snapped her head around in the direction of the fetid stench and zeroed in on the culprit with her telescopic, stormy eyes. Positioned about two and a half miles away, in a mountain crevasse overlooking the forested valley, was a Sinteverete archer. The foul wizard, wearing a disgusting and offensive necklace of Pentavi yaggowar teeth, had a charmed arrow pointed directly at the bock she was hunting. He sensed her gaze and smirked a smarmy smile while winking. He let loose the arrow, and it sang through the air like a swallow.

Maysiff roared loudly and alerted the beast to her presence, sending it galloping away before the arrow could meet its heart. In a flash, the Sinteverete archer appeared directly in front of her, in his tight, maroon leather suit and flapping black hood. With an outraged look, he drew his bow and arrow. She towered over him like a cat with a mouse, grinding her teeth in mirrored anger. The two of them stood in a stalemate for a very long time before the warlock finally stiffened, relaxed his bow and lowered it. "You fucking Pentavi pussycats are all the same. You're missing a leash, bitch."

Maysiff lowered her massive head to the warlock's eye and growled fiercely into his face.

"Lord, have you been eating skunk or what?" He said, waving his hand in front of his nose.

Maysiff transformed back into a naked female, her fiery red hair tangling within her Ceridome wraps as they crisscrossed themselves over her body while the Sinteverete archer looked on with greasy interest.

Maysiff growled, "You best pull your eyeballs off me, warlock. I realize it has been many millennia since you've seen a pussy...cat, but I have no time for your peasant humor."

"Got somewhere you need to be? You're late for dinner, that's for sure. You've blown that for both of us." The mage continued to stare at her breasts while talking.

"Better no one eats than a sneak thief like you," Maysiff huffed. "Have you no honor, troll?"

The warlock scoffed, "I proffer no honor to the honorless, cun-"

Maysiff cut him off before he could complete his unseamly comment, "Good talk." She grabbed her things and walked in the opposite direction.

The Sinteverete archer glowered after her for a lingering moment, "Miserable animal," and walked in the other direction.

Maysiff indignantly walked the path of Rosh Simbique towards her clan's land when she noticed another Sinteverete male walking the path toward her. A great sigh escaped her lips. Must she suffer another encounter with Sinteverete scum in less than a few hours? Is once in a hundred years not enough? Her hackles raised, and her temperament plunged. She was in no mood for any Sinteverete bullshit that night. Her stomach hungrily complained as if reminding her of how angry she was from before.

Then she had another thought. She was overwhelmingly tired of hating them. Carrying around this much contempt for people was exhausting. She rarely had to endure anyone from the Sinteverete clan this far out in the valleys anyway, so she decided she would do something completely unheard of, she was going to be the better person and offer the warlock one small gesture of mutual respect. Maybe said small gesture could change the realms.

Maysiff started to smile a very small, naive, but inconspicuous smile to herself. She felt good about this epiphany. Maybe the sentiment would catch on! What should she do? A smile, or a wave, perhaps?

No, he would assume she was being disingenuous. Maybe saying "hello" would suffice? No, she didn't want to directly address the mage, knowing he would consider it an insult and assume she was trying to antagonize him. Suddenly, she had it. A slight nod of her head in his direction would convey everything she wanted to say in a subtle, kind gesture without risking the wrong reaction. She was excited.

As the Sinteverete male grew closer, she could read disgust on his face. No matter, she thought triumphantly, she was still going to nod politely to him. Maysiff felt nervous but invigorated as the distance between them closed. He was almost upon her...and, NOW.

Maysiff respectfully nodded her head ever so slightly in the direction of the Sinteverete sorcerer as he sauntered by her, but the snarky sorcerer did not return her offering of respect. He clearly saw her unbelievably colossal act of unparalleled charity but chose to snub her coldly with a snort and an eye roll instead of reciprocating.

Now, Maysiff had trained relentlessly her entire life, as all Pentavi had; she was calm and untroubled during countless bloody battles and had gracefully taken down the most ferocious prey imaginable, but this—this unrequited act of selflessness tore through the tapestry of her resolve like a bull through tissue paper.

In an instant, Maysiff transformed into her sleek, deadly yaggowar form and was upon the unsuspecting Sinteverete clansman before he could muster a defense. She effortlessly tore off his right arm, known to be the Sinteverete's spell-casting hand, and tossed it into the woods like an old shoe. The clansman bellowed in agony as Maysiff turned her teeth to his throat.

She clamped her massive maw around the soft, pale flesh of his neck and devoured it in genuine hunger. Deep red blood bathed her wrinkled snout and rained down around her like a spring shower. She buried her muzzle deep inside the wound until she found his black, beating heart. He screamed unnaturally, the sound of air leaving the tattered remnants of his ruined vocal cords in a guttural yelp. Maysiff mauled and shredded his body in order to greedily gulp down the flesh more efficiently. She completely devoured him down to the bone in a matter of moments but was still hungry.

She paused in a microsecond, hearing a ruckus up ahead. Maysiff focused her telescopic eyes through the darkness and caught sight of 11 Sinteverete clansmen moving in quickly through the fireflies to investigate. Fuck sake. Over a hundred years with no Sinteverete contact, and here's a damn baker's dozen in one fucking day. They must be running out of wild game on their land to be hunting in neutral territory so conspicuously. She hoped they were starving.

The squad of Sinteveretes was right over the hill now, nothing for Maysiff to do but crouch silently in the darkness by the forest line. They converged on the remains of their clansman and swiftly began investigating.

Maysiff knew she had to make a decision right then as to whether or not she would try to take them all out or escape. Once they had a little more time with the body, they would know exactly what had happened. It was desperately obvious that a Pentavie yaggowar mauled him. The bites and claw marks were all telltale signs, and the other Sinteverete fucker that she had run into earlier would connect the dots no doubt. She had to kill them all and get rid of their corpses or risk them declaring war. No small task. She wondered if she would be able to eat that many men, but she was willing to try.

It figured, instead of bringing the clans together through some grand gesture of respect, she had managed to threaten thousands of years of respite because some clown made her lose her temper.

No, wait; fuck all that. That eunuch deserved everything he got, and so did this walking buffet. She may have been tired of hating them, but she would never tire of eating their self-satisfied faces.

Maysiff suddenly lept out of the tall grass and began murdering the Sinteveretes as quickly as she could so they couldn't defend themselves. She made sure to rip their right arms off first, like removing the scorpion's stinger, before tearing out their hearts and throats. Within the space of eight seconds, she had killed all 11 of them.

In a flash, Maysiff transformed back to her Pentavi form and marveled at the carnage. "This may cause ripples."

CHAPTER 4
BEAUTY IS A BLADE

"Lord almighty, Maysiff. What were you thinking?" Layluna barked, demanding an explanation, her fierce green eyes flaring.

"They'll never be found, I promise. I ate most of them and dragged the rest of the remains down to the caves. The beasts there will make short work of it all, I assure you." Maysiff was anxious and rattled but confident and clear thinking.

Layluna sat across from Maysiff under the cool shade of a thorn-willow tree. The beautiful Pentavi land stretched out for hundreds of miles in front of them. The Cliversol mountain range looked like a wildfire raging across the horizon due to the myriad of fall colors exploding in season.

Layluna couldn't help but trust her dear friend and second in command. She placed her hand on Maysiff's shoulder, "It's okay; I understand how hard it is to tolerate those buffoons. Frankly, the fact that you politely nodded at one is the hardest thing to believe about this story."

Layluna and Maysiff couldn't contain their giggles, which quickly deteriorated into full-blown laughter. After a moment, Layluna composed herself, "Honestly, Maysiff, I should be thanking you; I was desperate to petition for war with the Sinteverete again anyway. I absolutely cannot stand those smug, overrated tricksters and their undeserved sense of self-accomplishment. They have unbelievable gall sashaying so close to our lands and hunting the neutral grounds so heavily. They are basically daring us to throw the gauntlet down. I wager it wouldn't take much convincing to get the Elders to support a...campaign of discouragement at our borders."

The two friends laughed again. Maysiff thought for a moment, "I wish I knew this before I spent all night dragging those fool's corpses down to the caverns. Otherwise, I would have just hauled them straight to the Sinteverete's front gate and scrawled a declaration of war in blood on it."

"Where's the class in that, my love? Your killing and disposing of the witnesses allows us time to declare war and plan a measure of attack," Layluna said, smiling and clasping her hands together. "Fetch me Beauty."

Maysiff walked the path through the Pentavi main courtyard, surrounded by ancient, elaborately etched stone temples trimmed with dark, rich cherry wood. Lush gardens of magnificent late season flowers bloomed everywhere; embers against the fires of exploding fall foliage.

Maysiff finally arrived at her den. She had been out hunting for quite some time, so the coarse, canvas walls surrounding the subterranean burrow were a welcome sight.

She pulled the flap away and entered, descending the long stone staircase down to the earthen floor of her domicile. Beautiful, intricately woven tapestries decorated the walls, along with shiny, golden and silver incense burners that sat coolly on shelves, waiting to be reignited. Maysiff breathed in the lovingly familiar smells and made her way over to the floor well. She dipped her hands into the frigid water and cleaned off the soil from her journeys.

After Maysiff felt more like herself, she headed cautiously to Layluna's den to collect Beauty. She was thinking hard truths the whole time and was torn between her own boiling hatred of the Sinteverete and being the catalyst of war. Even though she loved the idea of killing Sinteverete scum—a lot—she didn't want her beloved sisters dying alongside her because of a war she started. Initially, all she had wanted was to be kind and work through her anger in a positive way—try something different, but she figured that just wasn't realistic considering the history they had with the Sinteverete. She felt like a fool for trying.

Word of what she had done got around very quickly, and Maysiff had sisters stopping her on the paths, patting her on the back and complimenting her. All the girls from the gardens to the training temple were cheering her on and talking excitedly about going back to war with the Sinteverete. Some were even talking about declaring this a holiday.

All Maysiff knew was that she felt awful for accomplishing the exact opposite of what she was trying to accomplish. The hatred they all felt for the Sinteverete was an easy trapping to get caught up in, and things that were easy always made Maysiff anxious. The path of least resistance was seldom the right path.

Maysiff arrived at Layluna's scantily decorated den and found her war room. Inside was her armor, her weapons, and Beauty. Maysiff gathered Beauty, knowing exactly what this meant, but swallowed her angst and headed back towards the Elders' temple.

Layluna met Maysiff outside the Elder's temple; a large, electrified group of Pentavi had already gathered in anticipation of Layluna's declaration of war with the Sinteverete. Maysiff looked at everyone frenzied and cheering for them, but all she saw was boredom. Why else would everyone be so excited to kill and be killed if not for an insatiable appetite for blood due to millennia of complacency? It was unnatural for two predator clans to occupy space so close to one another without conflict. They were destined to clash and cause sparks until only one clan remained. As Maysiff mentally recited all the learned reasons to hate the Sinteverete, she couldn't help feeling like someone had been pulling her strings for a very long time.

Layluna gently took Beauty from Maysiff and stared at her lovingly for a long moment. "She's perfect," Layluna said more to herself than Maysiff. "I haven't held her in so long."

"She's gorgeous," Maysiff said more to herself than Layluna. "Captivating. I can see exactly why you named her Beauty."

The almost unassuming, elegantly carved, efficient, sleek white handle and blade were all made of the same indestructible Pentavi granite that can only be forged using ancient, high-level Sinteverete magic. Its surface resembled an unearthly, silky marble that nothing known to the realms can break. Only the same magic used to shape it could destroy it. This particular pearl boasted a short blade with a wicked curved end. The edge of the curve was so sharp it would cut anything, even Pentavi granite. Decorative bleeder holes were carved into the blade's surface, giving it a gorgeous but deadly design.

Beauty had been in Layluna's family for a million years; from when the clans were Zol, long before the Great Divide. A Sinteverete warlock forged it for his brother and his Pentavi wife as a gift to commemorate the birth of what would unknowingly be the last sanctioned Yasmani Ro child born.

"She is my protector, my dear friend, my companion, my confidant...and my declaration of war." Layluna stared at Beauty mesmerized. "There is something so special about her. On her polished surface, she reflects all of my strengths, as well as the world's loveliness, all while showing me what's at my back. She has my respect and my trust. She captures the true meaning and duality of Beauty. She is beautiful, yes, but she is also deadly. She is love and life, as well as sadness and death. She is indeed a beauty, and Beauty is a blade."

The seven Elders stood stoically with their elaborately beaded gray hair and backs to Layluna and Maysiff as Layluna prepared for her declaration of war. All interactions with the Elders were conducted with their backs to you; no one had ever seen their faces. The tradition was steeped in history and status but seemed incredibly antiquated and isolationist to Layluna and Maysiff. It always felt disrespectful to them both, who served without question or complaint, eternally. The least they could do was face their constituents, but apparently status and theater were more important to them than respect. Their ostentatious robes, dripping with gold and jewels, did little to diminish their feelings of inequality.

Layluna accepted how things were and would put up with much in the meantime because she truly loved her clan. The only thing lacking was the thrill of combat, and that was about to be rectified. Petavi warriors were already lining up, adding their names to the regiment scroll, praying they would be selected for battle.

"Step forward, Layluna," the Queen Elder spoke eloquently.

Layluna came forward with confidence, "Elder Queen, we have come here today to-"

"-Declare war on the Sinteverete. Yes, we are aware," the Elder coldly interrupted Layluna.

"Then you are aware that they are encroaching on our lands and heavily hunting the neutral grounds."

"We are. Carve your declaration into the Tablet of Tabanersmoth and mass your troops."

Layluna couldn't believe the Elders so unceremoniously authorized her declaration of war. Typically, they didn't enter into war so lightly. They had gone to war with the Sinteverete thousands of times before, but for every single instance, there was ceremony, ritual, Pomp and Circumstance; but this was...unusual, to say the least. Layluna inexplicably let one word slip desperately into her mind before she was able to force it out like a splinter: suspicious.

Despite her fleeting uncertainty, she knew blood and conflict were close, which eclipsed everything in her mind. She could barely contain her excitement.

Without warning, the Queen Elder spoke again, "I find it interesting that your weapon of choice and declaration is a stone blade and not a sword. Explain."

Layluna didn't hesitate to answer, despite the inquiry catching her completely off guard, "I prefer to be more intimate with my prey—closer. A sword seems miles away from the kill and far too impersonal. Finally, the blade is impervious to Sinteverete magic, does not require enchanting, and the stone is always thirsty—unquenchable."

This answer pleased the Queen Elder immensely, "Excellent. Layluna, you have always been our fiercest warrior, and your service to the

Pentavi has been exceptional. When you've killed for us in the past, we have always been pleased. We are hoping this campaign will finally end in victory over the Sinteverete. Once we have their Elders under the knife, we can invade the Earth realm and take what is rightfully ours. Then all the realms will be under our control."

"I will not disappoint you, my Queen." Layluna bowed her head in penance.

"We know you won't, Layluna. There is so much at stake..."

Layluna took Beauty by the handle, strode over to the Tablet of Tabanersmoth, and carved her name below the thousands of names before her.

Queen Elder announced, "It is done. Go to war."

CHAPTER 5
WAR

"Did you remember to bring it," Maysiff asked Layluna as they bathed together in the geowarmed waterfalls of Typress.

"Of course I brought it," Layluna assured her coyly. She reached over to her wraps, coiled on the side of the steaming pool, and pulled out a small, smooth, vibrantly blue stone. She handed it to Maysiff, who took it gingerly in her hands. Layluna wrapped her hands around Maysiff's that were now holding the rock. "All your worries and all your tears, go into the stone to remove your fears."

"You know just how to put me at ease, my love." Maysiff purred as Layluna held her hands tightly. "My mother used to say that to me with the worry stone before bed every night. She died so long ago; I can hardly remember her face."

"I'm here for you now, my love," Layluna promised. "I will never let fear touch you."

"Yet I feel it creeping in now. Did that declaration of war seem unusually...hurried?" Maysiff tentatively asked Layluna.

Layluna remained silent for a long moment as she tried to pull reassurance out of thin air for both their sakes, "I can only assume they are as eager to spill Sinteverete blood as we are," Layluna said softly, preoccupied with washing Masiff's hair now. "That said, this declaration was indeed...dubious."

"I agree," Maysiff confided in her as she gripped the worry stone firmly. "The Elders don't do anything without ceremony and theater. I wonder why the rush now." Maysiff seemed as though she were waking from a light sleep, and her words were gaining momentum. "This power struggle between the clans has gone on for so long, and so many have died. It seems like we are the last pawns playing a game with unknown rules. With no more children, our clan has been diminished significantly due to all the fighting and dying. Hell, the Sinteverete clan is suffering the same fate. What is the endgame here?"

"I'm starting to think the Pentavi and Sinteverete have done all the heavy lifting, eradicating ourselves so the Elders can stroll right in and play for real stakes," Layluna whispered, no longer preoccupied. "Is it so far-fetched to believe the Elders are playing a long game? I mean, a thousand years is like one year to us—even less for them."

Maysiff remained quiet for a long moment, "It's not so far-fetched, but the Elders couldn't take on the entirety of the humans in Earth realm alone; why have your armies kill each other and weaken themselves? You would think they would unite. Together, we have a real chance at taking over the Earth realm. It just doesn't make sense."

"No, it doesn't, and this fish stinks from the head." Layluna finished rinsing Maysiff's hair, and they switched places.

Maysiff set her worry stone on the edge of the pool and began washing Layluna's hair as the steam from the water surrounded them in cloudy mystery. "We better be extremely careful; we don't want to have any conversations like this with anyone else. They would execute us in a flash."

"Yes, I know," Layluna told her. "In any case, we've declared war and there's no going back on that now. I'm with you, though; I don't like what my gut is telling me about all this." Layluna was fraught with tension, despite the warm water, kind companionship, and relaxing bath. "We really have no choice but to continue on our current trajectory, right or wrong."

"Agreed, but I don't like feeling as though I'm being manipulated," Maysiff growled. "I would devour the Elders if I found out they've been playing us for fools all these millennia."

"For such a sweet, caring soul, you sure have a shit temper," Layluna joked. Maysiff snapped her head around to meet Layluna's soft eyes, "I'm only kidding before you get your hackles up. In fact, I say we use the war as a little fact-finding mission; what do you say?"

"What do you have in mind?" Maysiff asked, now fiercely interested.

"You'll see..."

As they stood and turned to embrace, Maysiff's worry stone discreetly slipped into the water.

Within the dark, quiet, barren confines of Layluna's den, she and Maysiff poured over the regiment sign up scroll. Layluna's den contained only weapons and armor among the essentials—no embellishments or frills, a direct contrast to Maysiff's elaborately decorated and welcoming den.

They smoked a wrap of deadman leaves while Layluna furrowed her brow in concentration. Maysiff read her reaction, "What is it?"

"Every single Pentavi woman in the clan has signed up to join us in our glorious battle," Layluna said softly.

"Isn't that exactly what you expected?" Maysiff asked curiously.

"It is."

"So…" Maysiff grew impatient. "Spit it out, Layluna. What's up?"

"There are only ten thousand of us left…" Layluna trailed off.

Maysiff stared at her in disbelief. "Oh, my Lord," Maysiff managed, the wind leaving her sails. "That can't be…"

"It is; I've triple checked it. We are down to the last ten thousand of our precious Pentavi sisters—minus the seven Elders, of course."

"How many Pentavi did we lose in the last war?" Maysiff asked, her voice crackling with burgeoning tears.

"Twenty thousand," Layluna whispered. "*Twenty*…thousand…"

"Lord. How could I have been so aloof about it all?" Maysiff finally broke down.

"I can't believe five days ago, it was the highest honor to die in battle; now…it just feels like sending people I love into a meat grinder. I have to pull a thousand warriors to fill a minimum regiment of fighters." Layluna put her head in her hands and wept with Maysiff. "We've been such fools."

"What can we do? We're back to square one. We can't return to the Elders and retract our declaration of war." Maysiff grumbled in between tears.

"And we can't go to the Sinteverete; they'd kill us the minute we stepped across their border." Layluna thought long and hard while comforting Maysiff.

The night seemed to drag on forever, and Layluna couldn't stop her racing mind. She tossed and turned restlessly. Maysiff was still in the cotton-stuffed bed next to her from before, "Try to get some rest, Layluna. We're going to need it."

"I know, I know. I just can't figure it out, Maysiff. Why kill your armies?"

"Maybe the right question is: what do they stand to gain by killing their armies?" Maysiff asked, rubbing Layluna's shoulders from behind.

Layluna took Maysiff's hand in hers and held it to her heart. After a very long pause, she answered, "Everything. They stand to gain everything once we're all gone. They aren't powerful enough to take us all out themselves, so what better way than to have us take ourselves out? It's not like there's any other way we can be killed."

"But what if the Sinteverete wins?" Maysiff speculated. "What if the Sinteverete have enough forces to finish us off, and we all die? Where's the gain in that for our Elders?"

"Where indeed..."

"Once we figure that out, I think we'll have our answers." Maysiff continued to stroke Layluna's hair with her free hand. "Even with answers, I fear there is nothing we can do."

"There's something..." Layluna began but quickly stopped herself.

"Better watch that kind of talk; this place has ears everywhere," Maysiff warned, kissing the back of her head.

"I love that you worry about me so much." Layluna rolled over, eye-to-eye with Maysiff. "I think you know what I'm saying too."

"I do...and I'm with you no matter what you decide," Maysiff promised and kissed Layluna softly on the lips. "I love you, Lay."

"I love you too, May." Layluna was so happy here with Maysiff, but this latest epiphany had her dreary and crestfallen. It was like watching the only world you've known for so long crumble and collapse down around you.

Maysiff caressed Layluna's face lovingly and looked unflinchingly into her eyes. They stayed this way for what seemed like forever, staring into each other's abyss, each woman trying to use her gaze to pull the other back from the ledge. Layluna ran her finger along Maysiff's jawline, drunk on her visage, and pulled her in lovingly for another kiss.

The kiss evolved into a passionate embrace, with the two wrapping their arms around one another. They intertwined their fingers and raised their arms, drawing themselves together, chests rising and falling in restless unity. Breathlessly, they pressed their lips together while sensually sliding their tongues over one another, stifling their moans.

Layluna felt Maysiff's breasts against her own, making her wet and wanting. She pulled one of her hands free, and explored Maysiff's body, starting with her trembling neck, moving to her pert breasts, until finally finishing down at her begging clit. Maysiff gasped as she became charged and hungry for more. She pressed herself against Layluna's hand and rode it rhythmically until it was drenched.

Maysiff cried out and came multiple times as Layluna skillfully played her body like a cello. Wanting to taste the climax, Layluna slowly dragged her long tongue down Maysiff's midline before raising her legs and devouring her insatiably. Maysiff began to purr and growl like a big cat as she arched her back in ecstasy. Maysiff exhaled a wisp of her Alma, and partially transformed into a yaggowar; her claws began to elongate, and her teeth grew into long points as she roared thunderously, succumbing to another climax.

Layluna lapped up the juice with greedy abandon, then bit Maysiff's inner thigh until it bled. The taste of blood combined with cum was enough to bring Layluna to the breaking point. As she continued to go down on Maysiff, she eased her other hand down between her own legs and furiously pleasured herself. She was so charged that the tips of her fingers felt tingly, almost as though they were touching an electrical source. Layluna began to shake and quiver as the tide of orgasm rolled over her.

Without warning, Maysiff turned the tables on Layluna, flipping her roughly onto her back and gorging on her sweet nectar. Layluna also exhaled some of her soul smoke, but only enough to match Maysiff, and the two ferociously toiled as though they were animals fighting in the wild.

Maysiff clawed Layluna and licked every inch of her, which was caught somewhere between beast and beauty. She eased up with intermittent gentle pets but then followed them with a firm bite or invigorating scratch as Layluna allowed Maysiff to dominate her. Their sweaty manes tangled together as light fur bloomed across the geography of their skin in reaction to the lovemaking. The air was thick and damp with their panting breaths.

The two Pentavi warriors knelt in front of one another, wrapped their muscular arms around their waists, and pressed together firmly until their mounds met. Layluna clamped her teeth down on Maysiff's pulsing neck to stifle her animalistic howl. Maysiff responded by digging her claws deeply into Layluna's back.

The two were on the verge of mutual climax when an explosion from outside rocked the encampment.

The two seasoned warriors were quick to react. They leapt apart and had weapons drawn in a microsecond. They remained naked, halfway between woman and yaggowar form, but ready for anything.

Suddenly, Yawnsee, a Pentavi Lieutenant, came tumbling into Layluna's den covered in burns and frantic. "Lay, it's the Sinteveretes. They're attacking!"

Layluna whispered to herself, "Those fuckers." Loudly now, "Yawnsee, you can suit up here with us. Afterward, rally the south quarter warriors and meet us in the western quarter. We'll try to flank them."

"Understood," Yawnsee proclaimed as she and Maysiff suited up. They chose the black seal-skin armor from Layluna's extensive collection because it was sleek, form-fitting, flexible and impervious to fire. More importantly, the suits were able to accommodate their Yaggowar transformations as well as their Ceridome wraps. Layluna, choosing to wear only her Ceridome wraps as always, quickly enchanted their armor with a modest but robust spell to make it harder than Beauty's Pentavi granite. Maysiff and Yawnsee armed themselves with fearsome serrated long swords and a myriad of poison daggers, while Layluna chose Beauty over shock and awe.

"Is that all you're going to use? And no armor?" Yawnsee was perplexed.

"It's all I'll need," Lyaluna was fiercely focused now.

Another explosion ripped through the canvas covering of Layluna's den and scorched three hundred square feet of their gorgeous land above.

Layluna, Maysiff and Yawnsee soared up through the smoke like fiery phoenixes, eager to get some killing done. Yawnsee hit the ground running and raced off to the south quarter, slicing through Sinteverete soldiers with deadly precision; Layluna and Maysiff stood their ground, looking fervently for targets. Layluna spoke quickly to Maysiff, "If you have an opportunity, keep one of them alive—discreetly. I have questions."

"Will do. Now, let's make our way to the western quarter on the backs of these pricks," Maysiff demanded.

"A path soaked in Sinteverete blood will always be the right path." Layluna grinned at Maysiff.

The pair of Pentavi warriors charged forward into a surging regiment of Sinteverete warlocks who were closing in on them fast. They were casting powerful explosive projectile spells that were quickly devastating the area.

A specialized unit consisting of a hundred beautiful but deadly Pentavi warriors, known as the Roses with Thorns, joined the fight with fierce trumpets blasting. They were all in various stages of Yaggowar transformation and tore through the raging warlocks with salty hatred. Though the fighting had started mere moments before, the air was already so thick with blood you could smell the iron in it. The Sinteverete knew they were in the shit now.

Layluna and Maysiff dove headlong into the wall of warlocks now nose-to-nose with them and danced the Devil's dance of death. While all manner of bloody chaos erupted around them, Layluna and Maysiff remained elegant. They fought separately but also as a team. It was truly beautiful to see; if you didn't know you were watching a war, you might think it was ballet.

Layluna's style of combat was grace and carnage combined. She drew her targets close, breath-to-breath, and looked them in the eyes as she sank Beauty, almost sensuously, beneath their flesh. It was simultaneously delicate and brutal. What one of her casualties may have perceived as a slight caress, was actually a deep cut across their throats. They dropped dead to the ground before they even knew they were dead.

Layluna often kissed her prey square on the lips as their souls departed. It may seem cold-blooded, when in fact it was, but it was also customary in times of war for the Pentavi and Sinterverete to fuck while they fight; known as the Right of Copunocture. Layluna and Maysiff were in a monogamous relationship, so neither one of them ever engaged in the Right, but many others did. It was always consensual and seen as a part of battle.

Most of the Pentavi were paired up with one another in real, fulfilling, emotional and monogamous relationships—like Layluna and Maysiff; while the Sinteverete preferred to conjure their subservient, hyper-sexualized, partners out of thin air—then vanish them as they became bored with them.

During wartime, the only three things that were allowed were killing, fucking and dying. The Elders on both sides would cast a contraception incantation, making it impossible for the Pentavi to conceive; then, all bets were off.

The ladies of Roses with Thorns took full advantage of the wartime decree and salaciously had their way with the injured and fallen Sinteverete sorcerers. The Sinteverete responded in kind so the war that had broken out not five minutes before now resembled a blood-drenched orgy. All the lines were blurred; the massive snarled mass of flesh and steel found a life all its own and spread like a destructive wildfire across their majestic land.

Layluna wasn't having it. With a simple look to Maysiff, they had a plan. Maysiff did a ninety-degree about-face back towards Layluna, carving her way through meat, muscle, bone and blood. She stole a kiss from the severed head of one particularly unfortunate sorcerer, before being confronted by another. A Sinteverete warlock was suddenly in front of her, wielding one of the most feared weapons in their arsenal—the cursed Blade of Black. If you even looked at its ebony surface, your eyes dissolved and you were dead. Not just dead though, your soul and skill were then trapped in the sword, and accessible by its handler. The seventh circle of Hell was considered Heaven when compared to eternal servitude within a Sinteverete's Blade of Black.

Defending against it was treacherous, but Pentavi warriors were highly trained in this manner of combat; not to mention, Maysiff was far too clever and skilled to be bested so easily. She gently closed her eyes and drew upon her other keen senses to guide her. The warlock tried to beguile and bewitch her with his wicked words, but she was focused and impenetrable. He raised his Blade of Black defiantly as Maysiff brought her saw-toothed long-sword down in a violent arc—shattering it dramatically.The trapped souls within the blade escaped amidst a shower of sparks, and a deafening chorus of screams. Maysiff continued her downward slash directly through the midline of the Sinteverete soldier and split him like a loaf of bread.

Layluna and Maysiff were now back-to-back, defending their position admirably. Layluna, "We need to bring this party to the Reclon War Realm before our entire countryside is destroyed. It's curious that the Sinteverete aren't interested in wartime rituals any longer either."

"Agreed," Maysiff huffed. "Once we join up with Yawnsee and the South Quarter Regiment, we can force them through the portal to Reclon."

"Excellent," Layluna proclaimed, drunk on the blood of war. She captured the attention of a gore-covered Roses With Thorn's General, who was currently smothering a Sinteverete spell-caster with her clit while pushing her thumbs through his eyes. Layluna hand-signed her orders to push towards the Western Quarter, and the Roses With Thorns General nodded with grim understanding.

Layluna and Maysiff charged off towards the Western Quarter, stony and determined.

By the time Layluna and Maysiff arrived in the Western Quarter, Yawnsee and her regiment were already there, but they were taking a beating. Layluna and Maysiff were met with the sight of many dead and dying Pentavi warriors who littered the quarter like fallen leaves. Their unnaturally twisted and bloody bodies were heartbreaking to see. Yawnsee and the others were desperately holding their own but seemed relieved and rejuvenated upon their arrival.

When Layluna and Maysiff dropped into the epicenter of the fighting, the whole polarity changed. Layluna entangled a trio of sorcerers in her deadly Ceridome wraps, exposing her smoldering and beautiful body, then shredded them into thin, bloody strips. Maysiff transformed into her gorgeous, fall-colored yaggowar form and feasted on the yellow bellies of her foes. Yawnsee and the others, reinvigorated, brought pain down like a torrential rain.

Pentavi women preferred their Copunocture be with live, struggling, despairing Sinteverete soldiers who were on the wrong side of winning. They typically ate the dead—or the soldiers who were unable to consent to sex. The parallells between the Pentavi and Sinteverete's sexual appetites, and the issues that forced them apart were not lost on Layluna.

One-by-one, the once dominating brigade of Sinteverete forces were beginning to waver. The strongest and most defiant warlocks who were still fighting the long fight were now being corralled into a tight circle.

Unfortunately, the Pentavi's victory was short-lived; another massive platoon of Sinteverete spell casters crested the horizon. The Pentavi morale sank as they drank in the sheer numbers, thunderously trampling their beautiful countryside on the backs of giant, black skink lizards. Layluna cried out like a crack of lightning, "More meat for the beast!" This rallied her sisters, who all simultaneously transformed into yaggowars, and met the battalion of bruja men with tooth and nail. Layluna chose not to transform and join the feast; rather, she got into position to conjure the massive portal to Reclon. This would be extremely difficult considering the bedlam around her, but she trusted her sisters to keep the boys off her back.

Every time a Sinteverete mage got close to her while she was preparing her ritual to open the portal, a Pentavi yaggowar snatched them up hungrily in their jaws. Sadly, it was not enough, and the tide began to turn again in favor of the Sinteverete.

Layluna, fighting back tears as several of her Pentavi sisters met death, used Beauty's blade to carve the massive, elaborate symbol in the ground necessary to open Recoln's portal. She wondered if she would even be able to open it. If just a single Sinteverete was able to break any line of her hieroglyph, the portal incantation would not work.

The Sinteverete frontline was within yards of her hieroglyph, some with arrows drawn ready to dissect any line Layluna drew in the sand—so to speak, when a thundercloud suddenly blew in above the battlefield like swirling smoke, and a lightning bolt, accompanied by a blasting trumpet announced the arrival of the Roses with Thorns. The storm was a clever bit of simple, but effective conjuring by the RWT as a distraction. It worked, the Sinteverete archers pulled their gazes just long enough for Layluna to complete the glyph, speak the incantation word, and open the portal.

A great explosion erupted from inside the glyph, and a massive black hole began opening up directly at its center. Layluna stole a glance over her shoulder, and despite the undulating, blood-soaked orgy of chaos and carnage unfolding all around her, she managed to zero in on one salty sorcerer with his bow and arrow still drawn, aimed, and ready to loose. He was unbelievably wearing a necklace of yaggowar teeth and claws, as well as a smug smile—just as Maysiff had described to her earlier. He let his arrow fly. Layluna knew she had only fractions of a second and dove through the portal before the arrow broke its circuit, shutting it down like a switch. As she fell backward through the portal, her last image was of Maysiff tearing the head off the archer with her bare teeth and claws. She had two wretched Skinks wrapped around her, with claws deep inside her hide; then the image went black as the portal disappeared. She was alone in the abyss, and it drank her into its inky blackness.

Chapter 6
Fresh Hells

Layluna came to on the beach of an acid ocean at high tide. It was already painfully lapping at the edge of her cheek. Her instincts instantly kicked in, and she rolled away in the opposite direction—directly into the gaping maw of a giant mollusk creature. The shiny, ribbed shell, lined with thorny muscle instantly closed around her like a coffin. It was like being wrapped in caustic satin, peppered with steak knives.

She was done fucking around at this point and exploded dramatically through the first layer of slimy meat and muscle, then continued up through the impossibly hard, bony shell; the eruption sending chucks of cartilage and porous shell splashing into the bubbling, bright green ocean of acid. A myriad of toothy creatures and tentacles suddenly grabbed up the tidbits in a flash-feeding frenzy.

Layluna scarcely had a moment to look around at the Hellscape of Reclon before the familiar sound of parting wind caught her attention. She bent unbelievably backward and narrowly dodged a crude weapon made of wood and rock. It was wielded by a savage and scaly Reclon scavenger, who looked like eight feet of stacked shit, with a hundred eyes and as many teeth. It unnaturally bellowed as Layluna unzipped its guts with Beauty, still faithfully clutched in her hand. The other less ambitious scavengers immediately lost their balls and fled in arbitrary directions.

Reclon didn't offer a moment's respite in its relentless desire to end her. Giant, barnacle-covered muscles, sprouting from the shoreline by the thousands, opened their shells and pushed out greedy, thorny tongues that reached out to grab her with cartilaginous spines dripping deadly poison. She cut and danced through them artfully, barely having time to catch her breath on the dunes before another horrific grotesquery approached her with a hundred hungry eyes. Before she could even measure this new threat, she saw several impossibly gargantuan, monstrous, hoof-footed legs spidering and creeping through the noxious gas clouds swirling miles above. The churning veil of poisonous atmosphere obscured the creature's body, so Layluna could only try to imagine the unspeakable horror those eight legs were connected to.

Always swift on her feet, Layluna lept high into the air above the approaching grotesquery that watched her disappointedly with its many eyes. She plunged Beauty into the hard, thick hide of a massive leg as it came crashing down from the heavens like an act of God. It squashed the creature below like an ant and almost shook Layluna loose. She unfurled her Ceridome Wraps and used them to harness herself safely to the monster's massive appendage. Naturally, the gigantic, somehow insect, and somehow animalistic leg was home to a million different, equally terrifying parasites and hungry beasts that all emerged simultaneously. While the gaggle of nasties licked their chops, Layluna chuckled, "What fresh Hell is this?"

Back in Val Tebrae, the war was raging inside the Pentavi's vast settlement, with no signs of reprieve. A large portion of the majestic Pentavi landscape had been turned to ash, which was mixing with the massive quantities of spilled blood to become a frothy, sick, pinkish mud that clung to everything.

Maysiff was fighting off Sinteverete sorcerers and skinks while perched atop a massive mountain of their broken bodies. Blood flowed down the cavalcade of cadavers like some kind of nightmare fountain, with Maysiff perched atop like a gut-covered angel. She had three arrows sticking out of her torso; one in her chest and two in her back, yet she remained unphased.

A Sinteverete fighter had his hand on one of the arrows sticking out of her back and twisted it gleefully, "Dying time is here," he screamed.

"I don't care if you kill me, or I kill you as long as someone dies." Maysiff turned to give him an evil glare.

"Not to worry, bitch. Someone is absolutely about to die," he bellowed, bringing his other hand around to conjure something terrible. "Stupid cun-"

Maysiff met his spell-casting hand with her sword and split it down the middle between finger number three and finger number four. The mage gawked in shock before she brought her sword back around and loped his head off. The sorcerer's body-wine bathed her black seal skin suit in strangely pretty, red accents.

"I like the way you die, fuck face."

Suddenly, the one fallen Sinteverete Sorcerer was replaced by five more, levitating to either side of her. One spoke, "Can you take all five of us in Copunocture? I think not."

Maysiff laughed as another two arrows struck her chest and abdomen. She continued to casually laugh as she brought her sword high and horizontally in front of herself and then sliced harshly down through the arrows, breaking them off at their points of entry like a boss. All five Sinteverete men suddenly weren't so confident. Maysif chuckled again, "You boys are like a summer thunderstorm; promise forever and never deliver."

They instantly dogpiled on her like a pack of wolves fighting fiercely over scraps of carrion. Maysiff fought with every molecule of her remaining strength but knew deep down it wouldn't be enough. She allowed herself a fleeting moment of doubt, thinking she would never see Layluna again or taste her spicy sweat. They would never replant the land or grow old together. Then she had another thought: fuck that. She snapped out of the failure fantasy and back to reality. Her eyes focused on the orange Sinteverete eyes that were only inches from her own.

He whispered like a cannon as his grotesque tongue slithered out perversely long and caressed her lips, "Stop this, lady. Proffer us Copunocture, and we won't hurt you anymore. We know there's surrender in you."

Maysiff replied back with a whisper that became a roar, "If you want me to stop," *a little louder*, "you're going to have to," *much louder*, "FUCKING", *screaming now*, "**KIIILLLLLLLLLLLL MEEEEEEEEEEEEEEEEEEEEEEEEEEE**!" Maysiff grabbed hold of the mage's wandering forked tongue and yanked it savagely out of his lie-hole. With a hand over his mouth, the now tongueless sorcerer scowled in bitter understanding that he could no longer incant. He and the rest of his Sinteverete quintet tried to retreat, but Maysiff wasn't about to let them make good their escape, so she blew them a kiss. The kiss enchanted them and froze them dead in their tracks. Slowly, they all turned to face her with wide eyes.

"It's okay, boys; I love each of you equally; there's no need to quarrel over little old me." She whispered the incantation with a wicked grin.

That said, the five warlocks looked into each other's eyes and began massacring one another viciously. Maysiff stole a smile and turned towards the frontline. A sea of undulating Pentavi and Sinteverete bodies, as far as her eyes could see, met her angry gaze. She sighed, knowing that no matter what happened, regardless of whatever The Elders were up to, there would never be any peace between the clans. In any case, there was no time for speculation, the war was beckoning her and she had no options but to listen. She swung her broadsword around behind her, clipping off the remaining arrows in her back, and took a deep breath in preparation of rejoining the fight.

"When I'm done with these fools, I've got some hard questions for The Elders," Maysiff promised herself. Gazing across the landscape of the battle, she suddenly noticed something very curious along the horizon—snow. It had to be over a hundred degrees outside, but there it was, on the skyline—a thick sheet of falling snow. She could hear the distant sound of rumbling, "Where's the hum in that...?"

The snow seemed to be fiercely blowing in on the heels of a fast encroaching black sky, that was more void than clouds. It was as if snow were falling from a black hole. Suddenly, The Roses with Thorns' battle trumpets sounded again, only this time it was their retreat song. "What in the name of unholy..." Maysiff began, but before she could finish, a freezing cold blast hit her dead in the face. Not only did it chill her to the bone, but it managed to hit the pause button on every last Pentavi and Sinteverete warrior going at it in the warzone.

As Maysiff tried to get her head around what this fresh and frosty Hell was all about, Zepull, a Roses with Thorns General, came running frantically out of the mix. She was battered, bloody, and missing an arm, "MAYSIFF, you...'gasp' gotta...'gasp'...GETTHEHELLOU TTAHERE!"

"What the fuck is going on?" Maysiff was taut like a spring.

"It's the 'gasp'...the...'gasp'..."

"Well, spit it out, soldier," Maysiff demanded.

"IT'S THE FUCKING NEVUSCAR," Zepull managed.

Maysiff sighed and shook her head, "I guess we're in some real pretty shit now. We'll just have to try and find a way to incapacitate or isolate them. Surely there's a way..."

Zepull overwrought, shouted, "There is not. There is only DEATH. We have to retreat. We have to..."

Maysiff slugged her dead in the face, knocking her out cold. She managed to catch her before she fell, "That'll be enough of that." She then placed her safely on the other side of the corpse mountain. That's when the hard thoughts began creeping in. Christ, even Layluna knew better than to fuck around with the Nevuscar. Her advice was always the same: run.

Maysiff looked across the amazingly silent battlefield from her lofty position and marveled as the unusually quiet sea of Sinteverete and Pentavi warriors parted. And there they were - the seven Nevuscar—The Undying—strolling smartly in their Nevuscar Absence of Light cloaks and red leathers, right up the middle of the separated fighters. The only one not wearing a cloak and leathers was the Wrecking Ball. He was an absolute mountain of a man at twelve feet tall. Completely hairless and almost as wide as he was tall, this monolith was so covered in scar tissue that he didn't bother to hide his embattled body. They all walked on top of the dead soldiers like they were King

Shit of Fuck Mountain. It was so quiet the only sound was their footfalls and the falling snow.

The lead Nevuscar, known to every Pentavi and Sinteverete still alive as Vasser the Voracious, mosied directly up to the base of corpse mountain. He slowly pulled his hood down, his long hair, platinum white, lost against the alabaster skin of his face. The effect made it difficult to focus on his visage. Red, piercing eyes like ember sparks looked politely up to Maysiff. He shielded his eyes from the blowing snow, "Cold out," he said nonchalantly.

"It is...*now*. Thank you, I was starting to break a sweat," Maysiff said playfully, appearing as calm as cool still water on the outside, but on the inside, she was an exposed nerve ready to explode.

Vasser nodded his head in understanding, "Indeed."

Maysiff couldn't believe how ruggedly handsome he was, even to her. She actually found herself entertaining the idea of Copunocture.

Maysiff, Vasser, the other six Nevuscar, and the entire frontline of fighters stood there motionless and quiet for so long the snow began to accumulate on everyone's shoulders. No one dared make a move until the Nevuscar did.

Vasser looked left for a moment, then right, then back up to Maysiff. After a minute or so, Maysiff finally waved him up. He conjured a crystalline sphere of light that enveloped him and transported him to the top. Once he was within inches of Maysiff and staring eye-to-eye with her, the sphere dissolved around him. Maysiff was very tall at six feet eleven inches, but Vasser towered over her at easily nine feet tall—give or take. Vasser spoke stoically in a whisper, "I sense an irresistible strength in you. If we were aligned, I would make you my mate."

"We are not aligned, warlock. Not to mention, that's incredibly presumptuous of you, seeing as though I already have a mate. And you aren't making me do shit."

"I sense that." He lingered a moment, "Is Cpounocture acceptable, considering your mate?" He asked. "There is no obligation of course; no force."

"I know. That is precisely why Layluna would not mind. In fact, she would be cross with me if I passed at the opportunity for Cop-unocture with the head Nevuscar. There is, of course, the expectation that I kill you after," she said seductively as foreplay.

"Of course."

Vasser spoke a few words, and his Sinteverete cloak and leathers disappeared; he was completely naked before her. She slowly pulled off her black seal skin suit of armor, then let her Ceridome wraps fall to the ground, now as naked as he. They stood this way for a very long time, Vasser lightly touching her wounds. He made a small incantation, and each one of her wounds spits out the serrated arrowheads, then healed before their eyes. All that remained were the scars.

Vasser finally moved in and very lightly kissed her on the lips. He moved to her ear and whispered, "It is our unfortunate position and destiny to follow our Elders, even if they are...wrong."

"That's an unpopular opinion," Maysiff said trepidatiously.

"I have no interest in 'popular opinion'," Vasser said flatly. "Maybe we'll get the opportunity to talk about it at some point."

"We'll talk about it *if* I recover Layluna from Reclon. I will do nothing so important without her." Maysiff began running her hands softly over Vasser's rocky chest.

"In that case, I will help you recover your mate from Reclon," he said unbelievably.

"This is far from the conversation I expected to have. You seem...nobler than your Sinteverete brothers," Maysiff felt strange complementing The Undying one.

"I am only a couple thousand years younger than our Elders. I have been around long enough to know when I am being manipulated," he paused, giving her a curious look. "A story for later. Now, if that's enough foreplay..."

"Eager is unbecoming of you," Maysiff said.

"My former mate always appreciated my eagerness," Vasser whispered.

"Former mate? From before the Great Divide? You are old, aren't you? Different from the others." Maysiff couldn't help the curiosity that betrayed her.

"She made me different...she made me better." A single, solemn tear ran down his cheek, proving irresistible to Maysiff, who licked it away.

"You are not at all what I anticipated as head of the Nevuscar," she admitted. "If this is some kind of craft or artfulness, I applaud you." She wondered silently to herself if his emotional display was all a game to ensnare her in his trap.

"Such shenanigans are beneath me, I assure you. We have our roles for now, but I'm very interested to see how this all plays out. If I am to be honest, I haven't been interested in something for a very, very long time. I applaud *you*."

Maysiff kissed Vasser forcefully now and pressed their naked bodies tightly together. It was like two electrical charges coalescing from opposing polarities.

As if to emphasize this point, a bolt of lightning split the sky like a white-hot razor and struck them in a shower of sparks. They barely noticed; their own electricity proved more intense.

Vasser looked down at their bed of bodies and thought better of it. He raised both his hands high into the air and chanted in a deep, sensual voice. In moments, a large transparent sphere of light, the same as before, enveloped them, and levitated them high into the air above the vast battlefield. Everyone below watched with transfixed eyes as the two warrior lovers consummated the battle.

The fighters below took a salacious note, and simultaneously everyone began engaging in Copunocture. The difference now was that no one was trying to kill one another; rather, they were all simply enjoying the sex.

While the largest orgy in history unfolded beneath them, Maysiff and Vasser explored one another with laser focus. Vasser caressed Maysiff's pert breasts while she worked his pulsing cock with genuine interest. She had never seen one so close before in her life but instinctively knew what to do. Without hesitation, she put him inside her mouth and was astonished to find it tasted like honey. This drove her mad, and her clit instantly became slick with excitement. She pistoned his dick in and out of her mouth, using her tongue as a friction source, along with her hand and her equally sweet but complementary flavored saliva. Her other hand she placed between her legs and gently pleasured herself. Vasser never made a sound, but his breathing told the entire story. He gasped and exhaled as though he were close to climax, but she knew he had the discipline to hold the edge.

Maysiff wanted to taste that sweet taste forever, but her throbbing slit demanded she put his manhood deep inside her. She let slip a bit of her Alma, but just enough to give her teeth and claws, which she promptly used to climb him like a scratching post. His skin was like Kevlar—smooth but impenetrable. She managed to open a small cut on his shoulder with her teeth so she could taste his divine body-wine. He reciprocated using his elongated, razor-sharp thumbnail, a Sinteverete trademark for blood sacrifices, and coaxed a small drip of blood from her flesh. He savored the drop on the tip of his long tongue as though it was from an oasis in the desert. Maysiff hovered above his eager cock, her savory juices dripping down in anticipation. Vasser grabbed hold of himself and pointed his dick towards her. She came down hard on him, climaxing instantly.

Vasser stood upright, Maysiff still hanging tightly to his body by tooth and nail. He clapped both hands around her muscular ass and found the end to the inside of her. She howled like a yaggowar in heat and succumbed to multiple orgasms, so intense she thought it almost easier to fight him than fuck him. As he thrusted orgasm after orgasm into her, he edged himself on the precipice of his own climax, fuck-drunk on the anticipation of the in between. When he couldn't stand it anymore, he laid her down on a thundercloud so he could paint flowers on her heaving, sweat-covered breasts with his cum. The twin suns were setting gloriously behind the black hole and its mass of toiling storm clouds that were still purging snow. The smoke from the fires created a purple haze that intermingled with the clouds and caught the light in just such a way that it was overwhelmingly beautiful. Vasser, always a giving lover, immediately re-entered Maysiff to heighten her pleasure before her last climax had even ended. He waited until she was coming again and came with her.

They collapsed, completely spent. Both of them were out of breath and fighting blacking out from the intensity. They lay there for a while like that. "Thank you for healing my wounds," Maysiff finally said, breaking the awkward silence with an awkward statement.

"I wanted you at peak strength for Copunocture...And you are welcome. You are a fierce force of nature..."

"Maysiff," she said, chuckling. "Maysiff," he lingered on the name for a moment, and a very slight smile came to his lips. "Layluna is a very lucky woman."

"Damn right she is," Maysiff said seriously.

"I am looking forward to meeting her."

"How many Pentavi women have you killed, and you can't wait to meet her?" That old, hard-learned rage was trying to creep in.

"I've killed two hundred and eighty-nine thousand Pentavi women, and yes, I am anxious to meet her." His eyes took on a hardened edge as he spoke.

And the old, hard-learned rage was back. "You're a bastard."

"Yes, I am," he sighed an old man's sigh. "Again, we all have our roles to play, regardless of want. Survive Maysiff, and we will continue this conversation. Hopefully, with Layluna. Perhaps the three of us may join in Copunocture after solving all the realm's problems."

"Perhaps," Maysiff teased.

"Are you still going to try and kill me now?" Vasser asked politely.

"I don't want to spoil the mood," Maysiff said with a huff.

"There may be hope for the clans yet," Vasser said in his own teasing tone.

That statement hit her harder than any spell, sword, or fist. She actually took a step back and faltered. "A Sinteverete optimist; never thought I'd see the day."

"I've always been an optimist. Ever since..." He faltered. "Watch yourself with the other Nevuscar; they will not share my sentimentality."

"Noted," she spoke quietly with a slight nod of her head.

The light sphere began to descend from the electrically charged clouds and settled into the nook at the apex of corpse mountain. A loud crack of metal on metal suddenly broke the impossible silence, and the war was back on. The sphere dissolved around them, and the reprieve was over.

Vasser's Sinteverete uniform suddenly materialized around him, and he turned to leave.

"I never thought I would equate any Sinteverete with the word honorable, much less the leader of the *dreaded* Nevuscar. Vasser the Voracious indeed," Maysiff poked fun at the immortal warrior.

"Don't let it get around." He chuckled in spite of himself.

She didn't have to see his face to know he was smiling. Well, what do you know about that, Maysiff thought strangely to herself as Vasser jumped down from the great height.

Before Maysiff could even consider jumping down, there was another quintet of Sinteverete hopefuls levitating up to her position. "Copunocture?" They asked in unison. She laughed, then split the larger one from scalp to taint with her Ceridome wraps as they coalesced around her naked form. The other four attacked, but Maysiff made short work of them, all while dressing back up into her black seal skin suit.

As Maysiff's mountain of bodies continued to grow, her mind was elsewhere. She hoped Layluna had made it to Reclon—and survived. Her one true love being alone in the wretched war realm made Maysiff's heart sink. No time for tears, though.

Without warning, the corpse mountain suddenly detonated dramatically, throwing Maysiff explosively from her perch. Still smoking, she crashed down harshly into the center of the battlefield. As she shook herself back to reality she saw Vasser's massive wrecking ball of a Nevuscar staring down at her with glowering eyes. He was naked as a babe, covered entirely from head to toe in thick scar tissue upon scar tissue. He was repulsive, and it looked like his dick had been chopped off long ago; all that remained was a thick, girthy stub.

He spoke in a gravely, throaty voice, "Hello there, petal. Aren't you every bit the beauty they all said you were." He caught her staring at his stub and smiled a nightmarish smile, "I can do a lot with this awful inch, my dear."

Maysiff stiffened and dropped her sword to her side. She began to laugh hysterically and pointed at his absence of cock.

"Shut the fuck up," he said, his disposition souring.

To this, she scream-laughed at him with such volume and venom that he charged her like a mindless bull, unwittingly giving her the upper hand. She pirouetted out of the way like a dancer and loped his right arm off at the elbow.

He bellowed in anger and frustration as he bent over to collect the severed appendage. "You're gonna pay for that." He reattached his arm, and it sealed back together functionally. He wiggled his fingers as if to demonstrate.

"Why didn't you do that with your dick, dummy?" She quipped quizzically.

"It got...bit off, and...digested." He said, no shame.

"I'm not going to laugh; that fruit is too low hanging. Sorry, poor analogy." Maysiff could barely contain her grin.

"It's alright; I've heard it all before. Ready?"

"Ready," she gave him a little nod and a flick of her wrist.

He charged her again, only this time he was ready for her. Maysiff brought her long, serrated sword around in a deadly arc, only to have the Wrecking Ball catch it in his teeth. She couldn't lie; she was surprised as fuck. He bit down hard and shattered a third of the blade, leaving it jagged and half its size. He proceeded to chew the bits of metal shrapnel in his mouth and swallowed them thickly with a grin.

Maysiff inspected her fractured blade, "Well, I guess that evens things up a bit, doesn't it, shorty?"

"Agreed. Ready?"

Chuckling to herself, she replied, "Ready."

He charged her again, and she sank the jagged end of her remaining sword deep into his heart, all the way to the hilt. They were breath-to-breath now, and he stole a kiss. "I'll be thinkin' about ya when my boys run the chain on ya, petal."

"That'll be the day," Maysiff barked, focusing on the fight now instead of distracting herself with witty banter. She let a large portion of her Alma out, partially transforming into a yaggowar, and met his size. She pushed hard on the blade and forced him back several yards.

"Surely you know you can't kill me," he said smugly.

"I'm not trying to kill you," she responded with an animalistic growl.

Suspicion etched itself across the roadmap of his ruined face, and the Wrecking Ball managed a glance over his shoulder. There behind him was a cliff that plunged thousands of feet into the rocky ocean.

He bellowed and dug his heels in, but it was already too late. Maysiff went full-on yaggowar and forced him over the side. As he plummeted towards the depths, she transformed back and hollered after him, "It's a loooooooooong walk around, stubby." Unlike the Sinteverete archers, the Nevuscar were unable to teleport, and she watched as he crashed like a gnat into a pond so far down below. She waved, "Byyyyyyyyyyyyyyyyyeeeeeeeeeeeeee!"

She turned back around only to see five of the seven Nevuscar—minus Vasser and the Wrecking Ball, of course—and an entire battalion of Sinteverete warlocks staring her down. She looked desperately for any help, but all the other Pentavi warriors, along with what was left of the Roses with Thorns, had their hands full.

"Okay, who's next?" She jokingly asked while slapping her chest with the remnants of her shattered sword. They all began to smile, but it was short-lived, and their smiles began to fade almost as fast as they had materialized.

Directly behind Maysiff—within the void between the cliff, sky, and ocean—a massive blackhole portal opened up, bigger than anything any of them had ever seen. It dwarfed the Nevuscar portal in size and was still growing. Suddenly, a massive and monstrous, somehow half-insect, half-animal leg came reaching out of the portal like a doomsday beast. The unholy behemoth being pulled out of the portal with that leg was truly horrific and spectacular. With no poisonous clouds to obfuscate it, the beast was revealed as it squeezed through the many-miles-wide portal. The creature had three horrible heads that could only be described as looking like skinned oxen skulls, with tenuous muscle stretched across each rictus like chewed bubble gum.

Each head had two eyes with no lids that constantly searched for food in opposing directions like a chameleon, and rows of jagged, thin, sharp teeth like a piranha lined their mouths. The massive titan seemed to defy description in so many ways.

It was a combination of many things that seemed unnaturally forced together. The eight legs had a hard, insect shell with long shiny spines and hairs, and many segments like a spider or crab, but the further you moved down the leg, there was long shaggy hair that covered a massive hoove. Impossibly long tongues with bony barbs at the end snaked out of their nightmarish mouths and similar tentacles dangled from its abdomen, toiling and grabbing at anything that moved. The goddamn thing made Maysiff nauseous just to look at. As she drank it all in, she noticed at the top of one of the heads was...a figure riding it. "What the fuck...?" Maysiff transformed her eyes into yaggowar eyes and magnified in on the individual. It was Layluna. She was using her Ceridome wraps like a horse's bridle, bit and reins to ride the beast into battle.

The gargantuan legs came crashing down all around them like bombs, sending Pentavi and Sinteverete fighters scattering in all directions. Layluna maneuvered the beast behind the battlefield and began pushing all the fighters towards the portal to Reclon. "Clever girl," Maysiff said aloud. Instantly every Pentavi woman transformed into a yaggowar and worked with the titan to push the warlocks forward. There were really no other options but to flee towards the Recoln portal.

Layluna searched desperately down below with her yaggowar eyes to try and locate Maysiff. "Come on, my love, where are you?" And just like that, there she was, waving up to her from miles below. They smiled at one another, but a quintet of Sinteverete sorcerers were suddenly in Layluna's personal space. She hated the ones that teleported. With one hand, she continued to lead the titan, and with the other, she beckoned them with Beauty, "Say when."

One of the warlocks unloaded on her with a magical crossbow that fired ten arrows at a time, but she swatted the bolts away effortlessly with Beauty, drawing them in closer.

Without warning, a massive blowhole in the back of the beast opened up and geysered a foul, corrosive, fetid green liquid directly under their feet. Screaming in agony, the quintet was quickly liquified on the spot. "Yeah, gotta watch out for those blowholes, fellas."

Turning her attention back to driving the titan, she got tickled at stomping on Sinteverete fighters like ants. They were throwing all sorts of magic at the creature but weren't having much of an effect on it due to its sheer size. It wouldn't take them long to figure something out, though, which was why she had to herd them into Recoln as fast as possible. From her position on the main head, she suddenly saw a Nevuscar warrior using a huge knife and ax to climb the titan's left side head. Uh oh. He had red, coppery hair and lots of scars, but nowhere near as many as some of the other Nevuscar, which meant he was much higher in rank. He zeroed in on her and began stomping toward her. Fortunately, a long pink tongue wrapped around him like an oversized anaconda and reeled him towards the gnashing teeth inside its horrendous head. He managed to stop it for a moment but was quickly swallowed whole. Curious, Layluna wondered how a Nevuscar would fare being digested and reconstituted endlessly in the belly of this hellish beast. As if to answer her, the titan projectile puked the Nevuscar warrior out like a bad seafood dinner. She lost sight of him about 100 miles out. Patting the beast on top of its head, she told it, "Good boy."

It purred thunderously before its head unexpectedly exploded, propelling Layluna through the atmosphere like a bullet. As she soared through the air, she saw Vasser levitating in front of the titan, his hands still smoking from the explosive spell. She used her Ceridome wraps to anchor herself to the titan's other snarling head and sling-shotted herself at a million miles an hour directly back at Vasser. She tackled him out of mid-air, sending them both spiraling towards the earth like birds with broken wings. They fought one another spectacularly during the minutes-long freefall back to earth. Strangely the hardened warrior seemed to be pulling his punches. She used her wraps to cocoon him and reel him in close, "What gives warlock? Don't pull your punches with me, motherfucker."

Vasser smiled, completely throwing Layluna for a loop. He used the distraction to explode out of her Ceridome wraps. He then began to levitate, halting his freefall majestically, but Layluna shot out one of her Ceridome wraps and grabbed hold of his leg. It put the brakes on her descent at break-neck speed and snapped her around like a bungee cord.

She looked at him from upside down as he looked down at her from above, "Layluna, I presume."

"How the Hell do you know my name, mage?"

"Maysiff," he simply replied.

Layluna's eyes burned with an incomparable intensity, "How the Hell do you know her name?" She flipped herself around and began to climb tenaciously up the wrap toward Vasser.

"Cage your tiger, lady. Your mate and I..." A tentacle from the beast's underbelly unceremoniously grabbed Vasser and yanked the two of them toward a massive, toothy maw that began pulling apart in the titan's abdomen. Smaller tentacles emerged from within the mouth and slithered around them until they pulled them inside. Layluna brought Beauty up through the fleshy tendrils as though they were made of mud. They dropped her like a rotten apple, but she was still tethered to Vasser, so she snapped back violently. Vasser closed his eyes, said something and the tentacles dissolved from around him, freeing them. Vasser reached down, grabbed the Ceridome wrap, yanked her up into his arms, and propelled the two of them like a cannonball up through the belly of the beast and out its left-side head in a spray of ungodly abhorrent biology. From miles above, Layluna and Vasser held one another tightly. Covered in gore, they watched as the titan began to waver, its eight legs buckling, and the third head limp with its disgusting tongue hanging out. The mountain of a monster threatened to fall backward and crush the Pentavi yaggowars still driving the Sinteverete threat forward, so Vasser closed his eyes and chanted quiet words to pull the titan forward. The unholy creature slumped and lurched forward toward the Sinteverete, giving them no choice but to dive headfirst off the cliff and into the Reclon realm.

The titan collapsed thunderously to the ground, forcing the remainder of Sinteverete fighters off the edge but also crushing many of them under its incredible weight. Following them into the rift, on the back of the titan, were all the Pentavi yaggowars; thousands and thousands of them. They leaped into the void without hesitation, hungry for a fight somewhere other than their home.

Layluna looked deeply into Vasser's eyes, "Please tell me how you know Maysiff, and why in the name of all that is holy would you do that to your own clan?"

"They know the risk surrounding war. It was...*dishonorable* to pick a fight on your land. As for Maysiff, she and I enjoyed Copunocture and briefly discussed how I may be able to help the two of you."

"Well, that's a lot to put my head around. Where to start? Oh yes, *you*, help *us*? Explain, please." The Sinteveret Nevuscar smiled slightly at the corner of his lips. Layluna huffed and cocked her head, "In addition to Maysiff, I can smell that you mean me no harm. What the Hell kind of traitor or ally or whatever are you?"

"I am a friend...of sorts." Vasser let go of Layluna, but she continued to hover in the air with him. He chanted some words, and the transparent light sphere materialized around them. She backed slightly away as he spoke, "I tend to believe our Elders' plans aren't in the best interest of our clan. I suspect you may have the same issue with The Elders of your clan as well. Not to mention, I was always under the impression that our clans were better together than apart. Stronger. I haven't put all the pieces together yet, but this...hasty declaration of war has spurned my suspicions. Now I need proof, which is precisely why I have chosen to speak to you and Maysiff. I can sense your angst from a mile away. Better watch that with your Elders by the way," he added in warning.

Layluna's head was still cocked slightly to the side, "Good advice. So, I know you're telling the truth; no spell's going to cover that smell. Give me some time to think about what I want to do with that."

"Of course."

Layluna reached out and grabbed Vasser's cock through his leathers, "Thirty minutes ought to be enough." Now she smiled slightly from the corners of her mouth and slowly massaged his rising member. "I was too young when the Great Divide separated the genders, so I've never had a Sinteverete. I am anxious to dabble though...with the lead Nevuscar no less."

"I'll try not to disappoint," he grinned slyly.

"I'm not worried one bit." Layluna unfurled her Ceridome wraps, exposing her body completely and encircling the two. Vasser, for the second time in a few hours, vanished his Sinteverete uniform. She now had full access to his bare body and worked his dick until it was as hard as Pentavi granite. Layluna then let her Alma out just enough for a little tooth and claw. She licked him as though a lion might lick her mate and savored that honey flavor. Vasser reached down between her legs and delicately rubbed her clit until she was soaked. Layluna moaned, purred and growled all at the same time, her breath catching here and there. Vasser moved in and rubbed his pulsing rod against her swollen mound, and they both caught the same breath, her crying out a little. He looked deep into her eyes and saw such strength there; it almost scared him.

Meanwhile, Layluna couldn't believe how patient a lover he was and how he seemed almost a little sad. The combination was irresistible, and she couldn't wait to have him inside her. Vasser pressed himself between her thighs and started to hoist her legs up and apart, but she stopped him and backed away. He made no move to stop her as she turned around and bent over. With no words needed, he positioned himself at her precipice, but she reached between her legs, grabbed hold of his cock and used it to paint her juices across her ass. Without warning, she backed herself hard against his thick dick and filled her ass with it to the hilt. It was his chance now to let out a little cry as he had to force himself not to cum. She slammed her ass hard against his cradle and furiously rubbed her clit until she squirted uncontrollably.

They were spinning around in zero gravity, with no limitations, everything secondary now. Layluna pulled herself off Vasser's begging rod, positioned herself at a slightly steeper angle, and thrust backward, penetrating her pussy and bringing her to climax within a few strokes. Vasser put his cool white hands on either side of her hips and gave her no mercy. Layluna admirably took everything he had to offer but was still hungry for more. She pounded his pelvis relentlessly before finally pulling off, turning around and pushing him deep inside her mouth. Even that part of him tasted like honey; it was one of the many unexpected things that made him a complete mystery but also an open book. She couldn't help but hope there would be an opportunity for Maysiff and her to share him.

After a moment, Vasser took over, pulled out of her mouth, and dove into her pussy once again. He was gentle but firm and strummed her in a rhythm that continued to pay out in climax after climax. When he felt her starting to shiver, he pulled out, went down on her and lapped at her clit until she squirted in his mouth. He drank her, then pushed back inside her relentlessly. Within a few minutes, he was ready to explode, so he withdrew, and there was Layluna with her mouth open to taste him as he had her. He shot a thick rope of cum across her cheeks and mouth, and sure enough, it tasted like honey to her. As Layluna came back to reality, she realized they were still about 10 miles up in the atmosphere with the very last rays of sun disappearing beneath them. They began to descend back down to earth, and he looked at her peacefully, "Such an amazing sunset, yet I only care to look at you. You're stunningly beautiful, Layluna."

"Beauty is a blade, Sinteverete. Let's not go searching for the marriage stone just yet," she said curtly.

Snickering, he whipped back, "Your moxy reminds me of my first love. *You* remind me of my first love."

"Easy Undying one, you're coming on a little strong." Layluna caught herself snickering now. "Fucking immortal, and he's already trying to lock me down."

"I assure you, lady, I have no such intent."

"I'll just bet. Not to change the subject, but how is it you taste like honey?" she asked, curious how such a savage could taste so sweet.

"I bathe in a honey, lavender, milk bath every day, and I eat honey with every meal. Beekeeping is one of my passions." He replied, completely unaffected by her unbelieving stare.

"Fuck sake, you're more of a woman than Maysiff," she said, laughing outwardly now.

Vasser couldn't help but chuckle with her, "And there's that moxy again." They touched down on the back of the fallen titan and looked towards the portal, then each other. Vasser announced, "I propose we locate Maysiff, and endeavor to have a little chat with our Elders. Maybe we'll be able to save enough of each clan to start over."

"Dare to dream. You are an idealistic fool. I love it. I'm in." She smiled brightly at Vasser.

"Me too," Maysiff said as she clawed her way up and over the titan.

Layluna ran to her at full speed and embraced her roughly, "Oh, thank the Lords, I knew you'd make it."

"Of course I did," Maysiff said, squeezing her tight. "So, uh, tastes like honey, am I right?"

The two began snickering but couldn't stop themselves from outwardly laughing. Layluna whispered in Maysiff's ear, "He bathes in a honey, lavender, milk bath every day."

"Well, isn't that half precious?" Maysiff giggled, getting them started laughing again.

"You know I can hear you both, right?" Vasser said sincerely. That really got them laughing. He sighed heavily, "Our people are fighting and dying over there. Let's yuck it up on the way to ask hard questions of your Elders."

Layluna stiffened and snorted, "I propose we speak hard to your Elders first, mage. We're not so sure we trust you yet, despite your lovely honey and lavender scent." They all stared stony-faced at one another for a second before breaking down into laughter again.

"This is going to be interesting," Vasser said, inwardly enjoying the levity of their laughter. It had been hundreds of years since he last laughed, and it was more of a chortle.

Vasser conjured a sphere to transport them to the ground below, and the unlikely trio began their long journey to the dark, sullen salt flats of the Sinteverete's land.

Unbeknownst to them, Vasser's Wrecking Ball was there listening. A collection of gigantic, broken ribs protruding from the vanquished titan had a great big slab of meat hanging from the bone, obscuring the great big slab of meat hiding behind it. Wrecking Ball whispered to himself, "I never trusted that honey, lavender scented pussy. I always knew he was soft like a petal. Guess I just got promoted."

"Oi, Nevuscar. A hand?" Several Sinteverete soldiers were still alive but pinned under the quickly spoiling meat of the titan.

"The names Wrecking Ball, and I help those that help themselves."
Wrecking Ball stood stolidly as the three warlocks fought and scrambled to pull themselves from their carrion cage.

"We better gather some more Sinteverete reinforcements before
we go picking a fight with Vasser," one especially uppity Sinteverete
soldier proposed.

"When I want your opinion, soldier, I'll beat it the fuck out of you.
Understood?" Wrecking Ball bellowed.

The soldier bowed his head, "Yes."

"Still making friends with your amazing personality, I see." Bael,
Vasser's second in command, joked as he walked up. He managed to
hold onto handsome admirably but still boasted a vast collection of
scars. He was eight feet tall and arrogant as hell; even though he was
plucking titan puke out of his coppery hair. "Why the fuck are you all
standing around here with that dumbass look slathered all over your
features? Why the fuck aren't you in Reclon stomping the guts out of
the Pentavi?"

"There's been a...development, Bael," Wrecking Ball offered.
"Vasser has betrayed us."

"You can't trust a man who smells that good," Bael wisecracked.
"Guess I just got promoted."

The Wrecking Ball added, "He's on his way as we speak with two
Pentavi whores to assassinate our Elders."

"That's so Vasser; one sniff of pussy and he loses it. I have the perfect
prison in mind for him." Bael looked around, "Well, we have a quintet
of Sinteverete with two Nevuscar. I like our odds. Gentlemen, we have
our mission. Pull your thumbs out of your asses and beat your feet."

Chapter 7
Shifting Alliances

As Layluna and Maysiff followed Vasser to Sinteverete land, they had an entire conversation behind the sorcerer's back with their eyes. This could easily be a setup, and if it was, they were extremely vulnerable. Nevertheless, it seemed worth the risk, and they could definitely handle themselves.

Vasser suddenly spoke, "It's not a trap."

"Who said anything about a trap?" Maysiff asked in her best 'whatever do you mean' voice.

"It's okay; I would think the same thing," Vasser admitted. "The fact that you two are both following me into the murky unknown is very brave. You are fearless but calculating. I'm not certain if our roles were switched that I would have the same courage."

"You keep talking sweet like that, and you're going to make us blush," Layluna said somewhere between sarcastic and sincere.

Maysiff chimed in, "Seriously, stop being so nice; it makes it very hard to hate you."

"Well, I think I love the two of you," Vasser said matter-of-factly.

The statement froze the two Pentavi women dead in their tracks. Vasser stopped and turned to them with a face reading, 'why did we stop?'

"Are you trying to be funny?" Layluna asked honestly

Vasser flashed a slight grin, "Yes. How am I doing?"

Maysiff burst out laughing and slapped Layluna on the ass, "He got you good, darlin'."

"Not hardly," Layluna said, fighting a smile. "He got you too, bitch."

They all shared a laugh, and it struck Layluna just how improbable all this was. She knew he was being honest because she could smell it; there was no honey, lavender milk baths or magic to hide or impersonate that scent. She just couldn't believe it. Along their journey, she caught Vasser looking at a flower or animal a certain way, and she knew he was thinking about his former mate. She could smell that on him as well, a kind of sadness mixed with love. At one point, he caught a lightning bug, whispered to it so quickly you could have easily missed it, then set it free. How could this man be responsible for the deaths of so many Pentavi women? How was it even possible?

She abruptly asked him, "How is it that you care about unifying the clans so much but have killed so many Pentavi women?"

Without hesitation, he turned to face her and replied, "Because it was my duty. As much as I loved my mate, as much as I believed the clans were better—stronger—when unified, I swore an oath to protect my clan and defend it. That said, the oath was to my clan, not my Elders, and I fear they have lost their way. Not only that, but I suspect they have been conspiring with your Elders, promising immortality to them in exchange for their compliance and aid. It makes no difference what they promised or what spurious deals they've made with one another; in the end, whether it's my Elders or yours, they will turn on each other, and we will be long gone."

Layluna was vibrating now. She grabbed hold of Vasser and shook him fiercely, "You better tell us everything, warlock."

"Easy. Of course I will." Vasser placed his hands gently over Layluna's. "We should set up camp in any case. Sunrise is upon us, and we don't want to be out under twin suns on the salt flats. There's a cave with springs of fresh water a few miles from here that only I know about."

"We can go to your cave and set up camp, but I want to know everything that you know - right now." Layluna shouted while placing her hand on his chest to stop him from moving.

Vasser sighed, "I've had my suspicions for some time," he admitted. "The creation of the Eonian stank of attempted classism, but they prematurely let the cat out of the bag—no pun intended, and it fell to the people before they could take it for themselves. I suspect the provision of death during battle was a last-minute effort on their part to ensure control. Not to mention, it always struck me as odd that the Elders had us fight and die in their wars while they themselves never participated. I began to suspect they were getting rid of us, so I did some sleuthing." Vasser bowed his head in disgust.

"They'll never take the Earth realm on their own. Why kill off their armies?" Maysiff asked anxiously.

"I presume it's all a part of their long game," Vasser said solemnly. "I know for certain they have been trying to find a way to become Nevuscar themselves for a long time. As it stands, Nevuscar can only be bred, which requires very specific magic and a Pentvi womb. This is why there are only seven of us, and we are all male. However, they have been hard at work on a spell that would transform them into Nevuscar, giving them true immortality. They have been trapping Pentavi women and experimenting on them for quite some time, trying to figure it out. I recently...became aware of this and started putting the pieces together. I suspect they have finally figured it out, or they are about to. Additionally, I don't think my Elders could have trapped and experimented on so many Pentavi women without the help of the Pentavi Elders. I can only assume they have worked out a deal with your Elders for their assistance—promising them immortality, I wager. I speculate that they plan to replace us with mindless, subservient Nevuscar soldiers with a kill switch that will never question them and keep all the realms under their heel. Out with the old, in with the new."

"So why help us? You're already Nevuscar; there's a very strong possibility you'd be a part of their brave, new world. Why risk everything to help us, and fight a war you don't have to?" Layluna was desperate to put everything together and confirm what her wild mind had been suspicious of since they first declared war.

"Because it's wrong," Vasser said stoically. "Making us the architects of our own doom so they can create some kind of idiot warrior race to take over the Earth realm does not sit well with me. I was patriotic for a long time, even after the passing of my mate; I thought I was fighting and killing an enemy that threatened our way of life, but now I see it's just greed. Once you reduce everything down to its bare bones, it's greed - plain and simple. The Elders want everything for themselves, and they don't care what they have to do in order to get it."

"All their posturing and politics was just manipulation. We have to hurry." Layluna was becoming frenzied. "They are fighting each other to extinction over in Reclon. Do we even have time to try and hold the Elders' feet to the fire? What's our plan here?"

"I understand your being earnest," Vasser said, trying to calm her and Maysiff. "I have to hear it from the Elders with my own ears, and

I sense you need that as well. Once we have confirmation, we'll let their severed heads do the talking to our clans. Past that, it's out of our hands."

"He makes it sound so easy," Maysiff said, clapping her hands together excitedly. She read Layluna's face and quickly reeled it in.

Vasser also read Layluna's face, "Don't worry; wars like this have gone on for hundreds of years without any rest on either side, and thousands still managed to walk away. If we can save even just a few, we're winning. It won't take thousands to rebuild the clans."

"Well, maybe you can be cold and calculating when it comes to your own clan of clowns, but I actually care about my Pentavi sisters, and each one dead is a terrible, incalculable loss." Vasser gritted his teeth and began to look frustrated with Layluna, so Maysiff stepped in, "Easy there, honeysuckle. She's always salty before sweet. "

Layluna glared at Maysiff for a moment but couldn't stay mad at her. She slapped her butt, "Why not just tell him all my secrets?"

Vasser softened, "It's funny, but I actually miss this kind of back and forth. It's...refreshing."

Layluna slapped Vasser's ass suddenly, "We don't have to worry about Vasser the Voracious here keeping any secrets; he's a damn open book."

This got them snickering again. Vasser cast a light sphere around them and raised everyone off the ground, "This will save us some time. I can also use it to transport us most of the way tomorrow, but I can only maintain it for a while."

The twin suns were now above the horizon and the temperature already began to climb as Vasser transported them at great speed down to the caves.

"It ends here, Bael." Zax, the Sinteverete tracker noted as he studied the trail. "But we know where they are headed, yes?"

"We do." Bael tilted his head back and seemed to sniff the air. "I wonder where they will spend the day together. They definitely aren't going to try and cross the flats during the day's heat, so that leaves only two other directions - right or left. The water flows down to the right and into that lush valley. I'll just bet Vasser transported them down there for some shade and solitude. If I know that old dog, and I do, he'll most likely try his hand at a Copunocture threesome. I'd just hate to break that up and spoil the fun."

"That one bitch is mine," the Wrecking Ball proclaimed viciously.

"Have whichever one you want," Bael offered. "I'm only interested in Vasser. That Magus has some real balls on him."

"Agreed," Wrecking Ball noted. "He's been acting strange for a while now. I wonder what the hell got under his skin? To team up with the Pentavi, no less? I'll want to hear that story."

"Me too. In detail." Bael pointed down towards the valley, "Alright, Zax, lead us to them."

Vasser, Layluna and Maysiff arrived at a densely wooded area, thick with trees exploding in fall colors. The sphere disappeared, and Vasser walked towards the creak snaking through the area. He studied things for a moment and found the boulder he was looking for. He closed his eyes, said a chant and levitated the massive rock up and out of the way. There, below it was a rocky, moss-covered tunnel leading down.

Vasser brought his hand around and conjured a small sphere of light over each of their heads, "It's just down this way." He ducked inside and began the steep descent down through the passageway. Maysiff and Layluna cautiously followed until they emerged within a massive cave looking out over a plunging cliff face. They must have been miles up. The view was spectacular. The twin suns were rising on the other side of the mountain, so they had cool, moist air constantly blowing through the cave and out the opening. A steady stream of water ran through the center of the cave floor, offering them all a fresh drink. It was magnificent.

"It's beautiful," Layluna breathlessly said as she took it all in, her head on a swivel. She and Maysiff knelt down and drank deeply from the stream. Vasser subtly moved his right hand, and all the spheres of light over their heads coalesced into one bright orb that set down in the center of the cave.

"We should try and get some rest. We'll have to strike out soon and suffer a few hours of heat in order to get there by dusk."

"Mmmm hmmm," Layluna casually offered as she elegantly walked the perimeter of the cave like a cat, stopping at the precipice. Her back was to Vasser and Maysiff, who watched her quietly in unison. She began humming a soft song from her youth and stripped off her Ceridome wraps. She knelt down, cupped a hand of water from the stream, and poured it across the back of her neck and breasts to cool herself.

Maysiff cut Vasser a suggestive side-eye and began purring. Vasser returned the gaze and smiled that far-away smile. They both turned their entire attention back to Layluna, who continued to hum the tune while dancing gracefully. She danced as though the cave was a stage and she was performing in a ballet. Her backdrop was a miles-high ridgeline of forest on fire with orange, yellow, and red leaves everywhere. The deep blue sky had thick white clouds that reflected the light of the twin suns back at them like a spotlight. It truly was a majestic scene.

Maysiff stood, peeled off her black seal skin suit suggestively, and let her Ceridome wraps fall carelessly to the floor. She moved over to Layluna and effortlessly joined her in dance, as she had a thousand times before. They ran their hands softly over every inch of one another's taught bodies, all the while watching Vasser with narrowing cat eyes. They rubbed their heads together, purring and playing, then intertwined their hands and fingers as they maintained their sensuous rhythm and movement.

Vasser was entirely caught up in the provocative frolic, his breath increasing in tempo with them. The light from the orb on their moist bodies and the backdrop of fall foliage offered Vasser a memory he would hold on to forever. He tried to reign it in, but he couldn't help the feeling of burgeoning love for both of them brewing in his long cold heart. They were special, important, kind, but fierce. They both reminded him of his mate in different but similar ways. His mate...Zzoveigh. The thought of her name hurt his heart. It cut him to the bone to remember... Suddenly he was back in the moment, Layluna and Maysiff directly in front of him, each one with their hand on his opposing shoulders. He stood up slowly and watched them lovingly kiss one another. He began to disrobe slowly, choosing to savor the moment. When he was fully nude, they moved over to him and pressed their bodies to either side. He cradled them in each arm, Maysiff gently kissing his neck, and Layluna beckoning him down to her lips with her eyes.

Vasser leaned down and kissed Layluna fiercely, the connection charging him with electricity he hadn't felt in many millennia. The physical sparks were felt by Layluna as well, who gasped in surprise at the overwhelming passion. With her sweet saliva still on his tongue, Vasser turned to kiss Maysiff, the bond touching their hearts in a profound way. It was as if Vasser had been dead and buried before this kiss, which now woke him from his cold tomb with love and fire. Maysiff also felt the charge deep in her heart. The connection between the three of them was undeniable and threatened to consume them all. The link between the trio was not limited to physical touch; they seemed to occupy each others' minds as well, sharing in a way none of them thought possible. It was as though they were entirely in sync and operating as one entity, the realms all nonsense now. Two words struck all three of them concurrently like an arrow striking three hearts at once: true love. Vasser, Layluna, and Maysiff simultaneously froze—staring into each other's eyes fearfully, overcome with the sensation. They knew what this meant without any words. This was not Copunocture; this was not sex, it was lovemaking, understanding, realization—epiphany.

They succumbed to the tsunami of emotion and were tangled up in a love triangle. It was something to see the three of them individually operating in total concert. Layluna laid back on the cool stone, refreshing herself, and spread her legs like a ballet dancer. Maysiff eagerly went down on her, growling and partially letting loose her Alma. Her yaggowar tongue knew Layluna and her erogenous zones better than Layluna knew herself. Maysiff could never resist her flavor. As she pleasured Layluna, she raised her naked ass high into the air as an invitation to Vasser, who needed no invitation. He mounted her from behind and filled her. She cried out, ecstasy taking over, and buried her tongue deep inside Layluna, who answered with her own cry of pleasure. Vasser was reeling in the sensory overload; he actually felt vulnerable for the first time in his long life. There was always the idea that a Nevuscar could not be killed or hurt, but just the thought of them absent from his life from this point forward cut him like a blade.

The air was full of musk and pheromones, all of which churned them into a sexual frenzy. Layluna tugged and pulled on her own hair until she felt she might tear it out. Maysiff bit her inner thigh, as she was wont to do, and lapped at the open cut intermittently with her clit. Layluna grabbed hold of Maysiffs hair and used it like a restraint but also as a means by which to pull her face in closer to her begging pussy. She came like a fountain, drenching the warmed stone underneath her. Wrapping up Maysiffs hair in her hands, Layluna pulled her mate off of Vasser's impressive cock, so they could share a passionate kiss and stack their vaginas for him to fuck.

Needing no instruction, Vasser began penetrating them both intermittently, one, then the other, until they both came in unison like a tidal wave. At this point, the kitties both had claws and ferociously attacked the former lead Nevuscar, pinning him to the ground. Maysiff squatted on his face and rode him like a Reclon savage while Layluna sat on his towering dick, taking the entire length deep inside her. As Layluna ground against Vasser's cradle, she became enraptured in the experience and, for a brief moment, let the Sinteverete Nevuscar warrior into her heart. It was a second that lasted an eternity. She couldn't stop herself from the flood of feelings, so she let them carry her away like a leaf on a river's current. There was no denying the three of them had an explosive chemistry possibly never before seen in all the realms. Their sex seemed like a choreographed dance it was lovely, graceful, sensual and brutal.

Another climax racked Layluna, and she was forced to dismount and tremble. In an instant, she leapt on Maysiff, pinned her face down onto the stone floor, and began devouring her slit from behind. Maysiff reached out and grabbed two stalagmites and forced her leverage. Maysiff howled like a wolf in heat, and it was Vasser's turn. He picked her up in one arm, hoisted her legs over his shoulders, and drank her flowing climax like sugar water.

Layluna grabbed hold of Vasser's throbbing cock and deep-throated it to the hilt. When she felt him about to cum, she crawled up his body like a cat might a tree and sank his rod deep inside her, making her cum instantly. Vasser also came like a geyser inside her while finishing off Maysiff with his tongue. Without warning, they collapsed to the ground like a cut redwood and lay across one another, spent. The three of them were silent, but it was obvious that what they just shared was not Copunocture but something truly special. Clearly, they all had feelings for each other, but that would have to be a conversation for later.

From the darkness at the rear of the cave, a slow clap suddenly split the silence. "Very impressive, Vasser," Bael chided. "We arrived five minutes ago, but I just had to watch the master take on two Pentavi warriors at the same time. This undeniably seems well worth your treachery. Speaking of which, there will be a steep cost for that."

"You think the five of you can take me?" Vasser asked, chuckling. Tilting his head quizzically now, "Interesting." He casually pulled himself up from the flesh pile and conjured his uniform around his sweaty body. "Instead of dying, why not hear me out?" Layluna rarely transformed into her yaggowar form, but Maysiff enjoyed the intimidation and fear her yaggowar size proffered her. Layluna stood by Vasser's side while Maysiff transformed fully, towering over them all.

"Your confidence is...*cute*." Bael paced with his arms held casually behind his back. "I'm listening..." The other four Sinteverete sorcerers held back but were ready to pounce every bit as much as Maysiff and Layluna.

"I believe the Elders plan to do away with us. They are in league with the Pentavi Elders and intend to make themselves into Nevuscar. This war is a convenient platform for us to eliminate one another until no one is left," Vasser ground out, his anger growing at the betrayal.

Bael nodded his head and seemingly listened to every word intently. Vasser continued, "Afterwhich, they will replace us with mindless, tractable Nevuscar warriors so they may invade the Earth realm and have everything for themselves."

"Mmm, hmmm. That is a very compelling accusation," Bael admitted. "Any proof to back all of that shit up?" Bael was sincerely curious.

"I have seen pieces of the puzzle and put them together. Naturally, I don't intend to act until I hear the confession from their own lips - thus this journey. I know they will not lie - it is beneath them. So, once they admit their betrayal, we will collect their heads, and I will journey with Layluna and Maysiff," he used the opportunity to introduce them with his hands, "and facilitate them asking the same questions of their Elders. Presumably, they are as inflated as the Sinteverete Elders, so they will not lie, and we will collect their heads as well."

"I see," Bael said ponderously. "And then..."

"And then we unite the clans once again. We live here in peace, to hell with the Earth realm. We have everything we need right here. Why dirty our hands with humans?" Vasser spat out in disgust.

"If I may quote the humans, 'Jeeeesus Christ.' You put all this together yourself?" Bael was genuinely impressed.

"I have."

Bael nodded again, "I have to hand it to you, Vasser; you're no dummy. A honey, lavender scented man-pussy, but no dummy." He continued to pace but stopped abruptly, "We are Nevuscar," Bael suddenly shouted loudly. "There will always be a place for us at the table. The Elders have assured me as much." Shaking his head now, "You've had your tryst with this...miserable duo of quim. Now it's time to remember your duty. If you kill them and come back to the battle, I won't let the Elders in on this little indiscretion."

"I guess I owe you a fight then," Vasser said while pointedly pulling out Sepultura, his cursed Blade of Black. The Sinteverete quintet blinked in unison with black, inner eyelids that blocked out the blade's power.

"It would appear so," Bael said nonchalantly, his hands still held calmly behind his back.

The Wrecking Ball came out of the darkness and into the light like a hulking scab, "Hello, petal. Miss me?"

Maysiff roared in response.

Vasser stood informally with his sword by his side and looked deep into Bael's eyes, "On your go."

Bael moved so fast it was impossible to see, but Vasser, having known him for so long, knew exactly what the first move would be. Bael was no squirrely bungler, but he was a pompous twat that was as predictable as winter. Bael brought his right spell casting hand around like a viper striking and unleashed an energy rune directly at the trio.

Vasser cut through the rune with Sepultura, sending each half of the charged rune to either side of his position. The walls to the precipice instantly exploded in a hail of fire and stone. The trio held firm, unphased.

"That's why I learned how to whisper chant; spell casting with your hand is...antiquated. Please don't insult us, Bael. We can skip the peasant magic and get right to the fight if it's all the same to you." Vasser knew all the buttons to press on Bael to get him angry and unstable.

However, Bael remained poised and spoke colloquially, "I have played this battle out a million times in my head; I hope the reality lives up to the fantasy."

"This is what they want, Bael. For us all to destroy each other so they don't have to dirty their precious hands. You and this walking meatball may be Nevuscar, but these other three soldiers aren't." Looking at them now, Vasser tested their resolve, "Will you three have a seat at the table? I think not." The three Sinteverete soldiers never wavered. "Perhaps a place on the frontline with their imbecile army of puppet fighters. Meat for the grinder."

Bael laughed sinisterly. "You poor dope. Grasping at the ledge when you're already falling. Pathetic."

"You think you tracked us here, Bael? Fucking amateur; I *led* you here. This mountain will be your prison - your tomb, *Undying* one."

Bael slightly raised his eyebrow, calculating the situation, while Vasser whispered words, practically imperceptible, that carried a significant weight with them. A massive, intricate rune suddenly began to glow brightly under the quintet's feet. The three Sinteverete soldiers dropped dead in an instant, but Bael and Wrecking Ball were able to dive free before the whole backside of the mountain exploded like an erupting volcano.

"Please tell me we weren't bait," Layluna asked as Maysiff transformed back into herself behind them, the Ceridome wraps coalescing around her as the mountain crumbled.

"Absolutely not," Vasser promised. Massive boulders and rocks rained down, and the floor partially opened up beneath them. Vasser levitated himself and Layluna, but Maysiff tackled the Wrecking Ball before he could find his feet and dragged him through the black pit in the center of the cave floor.

Bael, buried under a tonnage of rock heaved the rubble off his back, stood like a statue, and brushed the debris off his shoulders. "Crafty," he managed. Bael was out with his Blade of Black now and pointed it at Vasser, "You always did belong with the women."

"Thank you. You don't see them turning their fucking land to salt," Vasser jabbed.

Bael was on them in a flash, crossing his sword with Vasser and casting a suffocation spell. The spell consisted of living, black sludge with tentacles that wrapped itself around Layluna's face like an octopus. She frantically clawed at the tarry substance as Vasser ground Sepultura against Baels Blade of Black. Vasser tried to conjure with his words in order to free Layluna, but Bael clapped a hand around his mouth, stifling the incantation. The two Nevuscar danced with their blades, but every time Vasser tried to incant, Bael was there to stop him. At one point, Bael even kissed Vasser full on the lips to keep him from uttering the words that would release Layluna.

Meanwhile, Layluna desperately pulled at the suffocation spell but could find no purchase on its oily surface. Layluna couldn't release her Alma with her mouth obscured and was quickly running out of options and air. With little choice, Layluna commenced eating the disgusting, writhing spell alive as it shrieked sickly. She put both hands on it and forced it deep into her mouth. Taking massive bites, she chewed and swallowed thickly, fighting the urge to vomit with every mouthful. Eventually, she had it small enough to uncover her nose and suck air into it. The last bite she chewed and spat into the face of Bael, who had his hands full with Vasser.

He smirked, "Classy."

Layluna exhaled the entirety of her Alma out all at once and transformed into the largest, fiercest yaggowar ever seen. Her striping looked like blood-red lightning against a shiny, panther-black sky. Her size was incomparable. Twin saber teeth hung low from her growling maw like two daggers, and her claws raked loudly along the stone floor like Hell's symphony. She was starved for conflict and anxious to taste Bael's blood. There was no question in her mind, she was ready to eat his flesh, muscle and bone. Raging, she galloped over to the main event and sank her saber teeth through Bael's right arm, preventing him from conjuring, and dragged him violently away from Vasser. Bael howled in pain and tried to stab her with his Blade of Black clutched in his left hand, but she shook him savagely like a ragdoll until he dropped it, then tossed him harshly against the jagged walls of the precipice. Dazed, he pulled himself up off the ground and winced at his broken, impossibly mangled arm. Disappointingly, the zig-zagging appendage snapped back into shape, and he threw a hex directly at her. It spread out in front of her like a giant web, wrapping itself around her. Layluna was tangled up badly in the trapping but fought fiercely to free herself. Every second she was trapped, the hex aged her. Her strength left, her fur grayed, and her musculature withered. She collapsed and threatened to die right there of old age. Vasser uncharacteristically bellowed an incantation so loud it made Bael clap both hands over his ears in anguish and cracked the remaining walls of the smoking mountain top. The incantation shattered the hex surrounding Layluna, then another calm word from Vasser's mouth and she was back to fine. The beast shook herself and roared in absolute anger. Vasser took the opportunity and flung a poison dagger at Bael, who still had his hands over his ears. The blade hit precisely, pinning the warlock's spell hand to the right side of his head. Layluna suddenly plowed into Bael's back at full force, throwing him face first into the rocky ground. She made short work of his cloak and leathers with her claws and began to tear massive chunks of flesh out of his back with her gnashing teeth. No chewing, she tilted her head back and swallowed the meal whole. Bael screamed and laughed at the same time, the combination extremely off-putting. The bloody ruins of his back quickly grew ropes of scar tissue and muscle, but Layluna continued to rip the scar tissue off without mercy. She was deep inside an overwhelming blood rage now.

Bael ripped the dagger from his head and suddenly made himself huge, slamming Layluna's massive yaggowar head hard against a rocky overhang - smashing it to bits. A jagged stalactite sliced a vicious wound through her right shoulder and bathed the three of them in blood. Layluna instantly shrank back to her lanky female form and used her Ceridome wraps as a bandage. Her mind was spinning, but Maysiff was all she could think about. It was pretty hardcore of her to take on a Nevuscar bruiser like Wrecking Ball. That's my girl, she thought with a smile.

Vasser was already soaring through the air with Sepultura and chopped off Bael's huge right hand at the wrist. A geyser of body wine from the massive stump drenched Vasser like a champagne victory. Emerging from the sanguine shower blood-covered, Layluna strolled right up to Bael, who now shrank back to size. His severed hand shrank as well but suddenly flipped over and ran like a camel spider on all fingers over to Bael, who quickly snatched it up and reattached it.

"I can do this all day, y'all." Bael was a salty son-of-a-bitch, to be sure.

"Gross," Layluna managed.

Down below, Maysiff and the Wrecking Ball plummeted miles in a fraught freefall, headed straight for a lake of magma. They duked it out like a couple of heavyweight bare-knuckle brawlers in zero gravity. Maysiff was still in yaggowar form, and the Wrecking Ball was actually biting and clawing her just as much as she was him. It was blood-for-blood and by the gallons. The two warriors chased their ruby rain through the air towards certain doom.

Maysiff slapped both paws on either side of the Wrecking Ball's head, and fucking ate his face. It grew back, but it was a grizzly, skullish rictus without eyelids or lips. Just when she thought he couldn't get any goddamn uglier—this. The Wrecking Ball pushed her away and clumsily conjured an ugly, green translucent glob sphere around himself. "Burn bitch," he sneered at her.

Maysiff pulled in her Alma like a puff of Deadman leaves and measured her situation. Still both in freefall, she looked around with focused intensity. The Wrecking Ball began laughing richly from his gooey glob sphere like he had all the answers. She unfurled her Ceridome wraps into a makeshift wind suit and used it to steer herself towards the far-off walls of the massive cavern.

The Wrecking Ball called after her ridiculously, "Hey. Where do you think you're goin'." He began running in the glob like a hamster wheel and actually got some traction. Maysiff glided over to one of the massive rock structures and used her Ceridome wraps to gracefully anchor herself to the wall like spider legs. Butter bean, on the other hand, kept running and managed to get to the edge of the massive magma chamber before splashing down. He maintained the glob sphere due to the immense heat but scowled up at Maysiff through the transparency. She smiled.

Using her Ceridome wraps like an insect, Maysiff scaled the shear wall with delicate dexterity and made her way back up to the main event. Below her, the Wrecking Ball stabbed his hands into the wall and began the long climb—staring at her the whole way.

Maysiff emerged from the cavernous hole right into the shit. Bael was holding back Layluna and Beauty with one hand, half covered in Ceridome wraps, and shielding himself with magic from Vasser's blade with his other hand. She immediately joined the fight in half yagowwar form, teeth and claws ready, with her Ceridome wraps a frenzy of fabric razor blades. Bael saw the scales tip and unsportsmanly shot Vasser in the eyes with venom from underneath his forked tongue. Vasser reeled, desperately wiping the corrosive sludge from his eyes. "Dirty fucker," Vasser hissed.

"Aww, don't be mad, honeysuckle..." but before Bael could finish his insult, Maysiff was on him like a virus. Layluna released him to get a better third person position and let Maysiff have a piece. Maysiff straight up out-matched him in hand-to-hand combat, being sure to occupy the right hand at all times. She was like a red-covered angel, the light now pouring in from the twin suns behind her. A majestic sunset overtop a massive ridgeline of colorful forest offered itself as the backdrop for the battle, and as last looks go, you could do a lot worse.

Vasser was back in the game with Layluna, "I'm tired of fucking around with this guy," Layluna moaned.

"Indeed. Let's bury him," Vasser replied in agreement.

"I love it," Layluna smiled with bloodlust in her eyes.

Layluna joined Maysiff and caught Bael in a three-way blade and claw fight. The sorcerer was admirably holding his own but was definitely adding some scars to his collection. Vasser levitated high up into the air and began to chant powerful words. A glowing sphere appeared above his head and began to grow into a small sun, eclipsing the twin suns in size in a matter of moments.

Bael saw the fight going south from below but had his hands full and was finding it extremely difficult to retreat. He suddenly closed his eyes but continued to go round-for-round with the two Pentavi brawlers.

Down below a sphere from Bael encapsulated the Wrecking Ball and spirited him up through the gaping, smoking maw of the mountain. He was back to join the fight.

"Yay," Maysiff mumbled. "You got this clown, baby?"

"I got him," Layluna winked. She tensed up ready to spring, but they all suddenly hit the pause button and tilted their heads skyward. Vasser was consumed within a fiery sphere the size of a planet. Layluna and Maysiff immediately leapt to either side, transforming into yaggowar form, and made haste down the side of the mountain toward the valley far below. The Wrecking Ball grabbed up Bael like a spear and threw him a million miles an hour straight at Vasser, his sword slicing the way. Unfortunately for Bael and the Wrecking Ball, it was already too late and Vasser unleashed the white-hot comet straight at them. Bael was instantly consumed and tossed back down through the mountain like a meteor, where he crashed explosively into the lake of lava, causing the mountain to erupt. Just as the volcano finally blew its top, Vasser's energy sphere crashed doomfully into it, collapsing the entire west side of the mountain face on top of him. There was no sign of the Wrecking Ball anywhere. The total devastation turned the entire area into a fifty-mile-wide open sore, bleeding magma and exhaling smoke, fire and ash.

Vasser dropped out of the air like an injured bird and plummeted towards the forest floor with a wall of ash and embers close behind him. Layluna and Maysiff caught the sorcerer with their Ceridome wraps and quickly reeled him in. Maysiff, in Yaggowar form, lashed Vasser to her back using her wraps. Layluna, also still in yaggowar form, ran by Maysiff's side through the burning chunks of rock and ash that rained down around them apocalyptically. They narrowly escaped the pyroclastic cloud of certain death that chased them at a few hundred miles an hour.

As they fled deep into the valley, the sun set behind a massive column of smoke and cinders; this day was over.

CHAPTER 8
A THOUSAND SCARS FOR YOU

Vasser dreamt of Zzoveigh. It was more memory than dream, but the context was different. They were sitting under a thornwillow tree in winter like they had a million times before, letting the snow fall and accumulate on the drooping branches, shrouding them in an icy igloo. She sat directly on the ground with his head in her lap; she was stroking his white hair and humming the same tune Layluna had before in the cave.

"It's okay, you know," Zzoveigh said sweetly between notes.

"What's okay," Vasser asked lazily, enjoying the tranquility of the moment.

"It's okay for you to move on..."

Vasser suddenly woke up like a sprung trap. He looked around anxiously in all directions. He was laid out by a campfire, Layluna stoking it with a long, crooked limb. "You should get some rest; it'll be morning soon. We're past the larger flats, but this land is still lousy with salt and deadman leaf. This is the edge of the forest before we hit the ridgelines."

"Maysiff?"

"She's okay. She's hunting for our breakfast. Hopefully, she can find something in this hopeless land. Are you okay?" She turned to look at him questioningly.

"I'm...fine. How long was I out?"

"Only a few hours. You're one tough old man," Layluna said, offering a smile, but she quickly turned away. She was conflicted about her feelings for Vasser, and this was all brand new territory for her. She could tell Maysiff liked him, which was a huge vote in his favor. In all honesty, she liked him too, despite her ingrained suspicious disposition, and her hatred of the Sinteverete. They had fought side-by-side, risked everything, and shared something...more than mere Copunocture, but Layluna's heart was still stone.

Vasser smiled, but didn't turn away, "I could have never done this alone, you know. You both fought by my side and risked your lives; I am forever in your debt."

Layluna stiffened and hesitated but finally relaxed and turned to face him entirely, eyes focused on his, "I was on this path as well, and running into you was...fortuitous. We make a good team."

"Well, look who's warming up," Vasser joked. "Guess I'm wearing you down."

Layluna stood seriously and walked slowly over to him, "You saved my life and Maysiff's, so you will never have to worry about us holding you dear in our hearts. You are special, unique, and...kind." Standing over him now, she kneeled and kissed him ever so slightly on the cheek. "I forgive you for killing my sisters; lord knows I've killed enough of your brothers. Perhaps someday, the killing will stop. Perhaps we are on the verge of a new day, one where we aren't pawns in a game where the rules have been kept from us."

"Dare to dream, Layluna. Having been the only optimist through-out the endless years, it's nice to see I am not alone." Vasser looked to the ground, "Thank you for trusting me."

"You make it easy, old man." They shared a light laugh, and it felt like spring had arrived. Suddenly there was a rustle in the woods up ahead, and the two quickly snapped back into warrior mode. Layluna whispered, "Up ahead, do you see it?"

"I do. What is it?" Vasser began edging Sepultura out of her sheath.

Layluna had Beauty out and ready, "It looks like..."

Maysiff in yaggowar form suddenly emerged from the dark woods with a large Bock in her mouth. She let it fall to the ground with a thud and transformed back into herself. "What?"

Layluna and Vasser began laughing again. Layluna chuckled, "Oh nothing, you just scared the shit out of us."

"Oh, sorry. You act like we're at war or something," Maysiff giggled.

"You did that on purpose, didn't you?" Layluna scolded as Maysiff continued to giggle. Vasser rolled his eyes but couldn't hide his smile.

"That's it, down there," Vasser pointed from the high, rocky and bar-ren ridgeline down to a massive black, round, stone temple trimmed with steel. It stood tall and dark like a colossal crypt. It was a mile wide and rose up a staggering three miles, with no windows or entrances. "I'll have to conjure a doorway for us, but I'll get us in."

"You sure about this?" Layluna asked softly.

"Of course I'm not, but there's no turning back for me. Keep in mind, when we pay your Elders a visit, and they see you with me, you'll be a heretic just like I am. Are *you* sure about this?" Vasser asked, looking from Layluna to Maysiff with questioning eyes.

"I've never been more sure about anything in my life," Layluna assured Vasser. "Those fuckers are gonna pay if a debt is owed."

"Damn right," Maysiff said, confirming her position on things.

"Let's go get some answers," Vasser whispered.

"Indeed," Layluna answered.

Vasser conjured a cloaking sphere to transport them down to the obelisk. The unlikely trio stepped inside and disappeared from sight. Inside the sphere they could see everything as they drifted down to the obelisk that was completely surrounded by salted land.

Layluna continued, "You're going to have to fill me in on the obsession with salt later, but first, I'm guessing, like our land, there's no one around?"

"Correct. As far as the salt, it's not an obsession...it is a toxic byproduct of our magic. It wasn't always like that, but the Elders have foraged further and further into dark and damning magic; the salt is only a very small part of the price we pay. We will salt all the realms if no one stops us." He shook his head. "I still remember sitting under the thornwillow trees, and beekeeping; this..." he held out his hand and put into focus the wasteland that was now the Sinteverete stronghold. "We traded all our beautiful land and the life on it for dark magic. We have all been such fools."

"We'll fix it," Layluna promised. "I am not naive; I am...certain. We will put them under the knife and heel if we have to. I'm mad as hell, and we're calling them to account."

Maysiff stroked Layluna's hair and calmed her. "I'm mad too, my love. We will have satisfaction."

"Truer words have never been spoken," Layluna said, a burning light in her eyes. They touched down on the course, salty land. The only thing that grew in cultivated, decorative strips along the stone and salt was deadman leaf. An ugly black and purple plant with thorns and pulsing, fleshy flowers that resembled meat more than flower. The leaves were nice to smoke, though. Rigid, twisted trees with no leaves and glossy, black fruit provided meager shade from the burning suns, which reflected brutally off the salt.

"I can't believe the size of this thing. So, the entire Sinteverete clan resides in there while polluting the outside world with salt. Shame on you," cried Layluna.

"I'm trying to change things—desperately. The only crime is complacency now. You are right, though; we will fix it." Vasser glared at the massive structure in contempt.

"Yeah, baby, lighten up," Maysiff cheered. "We got this."

"I wish your optimism was contagious. Can we take The Elders, Vasser?" Layluna asked, concerned.

Sighing, Vasser replied, "I don't know. We are in uncharted territory here. I will say this; they are us, simply much older—regardless of their choice of age. That doesn't necessarily translate into wisdom or skill. They may have grown strong on dark magic, but they are weak in form and untrained in combat. We can take them hand-to-hand. They can whisper chant, so be careful, forget the right arms and go for the throat. Once we have our confession, be ready."

"Excellent." Choosing optimism, Layluna spoke, "We're with you." He winked at her and whispered an open door into the smooth, black stone wall.

"After you ladies," he mused sarcastically.

"Uh, no, we insist..." Layluna held out her hand.

Vasser crept inside, "There won't be any Sinteverete here except for the Elders, but there are skinks everywhere. I don't have to tell you to watch out for them."

"Ugh, I fucking hate skinks," Maysiff groaned.

Vasser cut himself with his sacrificial nail and smeared the blood on them, "This will hide your scent, but if even one sees you, the Elders will know we are here. They share eyes."

"Great," Maysiff continued to complain.

"Lighten up," Layluna chided, pinching her butt.

"Don't start something you can't finish," Maysiff giggled as she swatted Layluna's hand away.

"Shhhhhhhhh," Vasser held up his finger over his lips. "We are close." The inside of the Sinteverete tower defied physics and logic. It was like an MC Escher drawing that baffled Layluna and Maysiff. Fortunately, Vasser knew every nook and cranny of the confounding, dark, glossy-black, stoney construct that seemed like some kind of twisted realm all its own. He continued to lead them through the maze of madness until they came upon a huge, sprawling room with elaborately carved columns stretching up to the high ceiling. The chamber dripped in Elder grandiosity, and the expansive floor writhed with hundreds of huge skinks. Finally, there were seven ostentatiously decorated thrones towards the rear with the backs to the front of the room. The thrones were enormous, towering, and black with red runes carved into their stoney surface.

Vasser whispered an incantation, and every skink in the room suddenly dissolved into salt. "Nice trick," Maysiff stated with admiration.

Vasser frowned slightly, "That 'nice trick' just cost me three grains of my soul."

Blushing, "I apologize; I didn't know. How many grains does your soul have?"

"I don't know," Vasser admitted. "When I've spent my last, I will become a pillar of salt for a hundred thousand years."

"Well, maybe stick to the lighter magic, mage." Layluna said coyly, "We're growing accustomed to your face."

Grinning now, Vasser quipped, "I rarely use dark magic; it is...a *loathsome* feeling."

A thunderous voice wickedly called out from behind the thrones, "Vaaaaaaassssssssserrrrrrrrrr! How dare you bring Pentavi women to our chambers. Impudent traitor."

"Them? Don't worry about them—worry about me." Vasser motioned for Layluna and Maysiff to stay back as he made his way forward over the piles of salt. Naturally, they ignored him with a huff and followed closely. He smiled slightly to himself.

"Insolence. We have a special hell planned for you and your whores," the lead Elder promised.

"Stop, you're going to make us blush," Layluna shouted.

"Silence in our chamber," all the Sinteverete Elders bellowed at once.

"Fuuuuuuuuck you," Layluna said definitely. Maysiff laughed out loud.

"You shall -" The lead Elder began, but Vasser cut him off.

"Shut up and face me," Vasser demanded.

Suddenly, the seven thrones, sitting atop a massive round stone set in the floor, actually began to rotate slowly to face them. The unlikely trio couldn't believe they were about to lay eyes on the Elders. The lead Elder, with the biggest throne, sat directly in the middle, with three other smaller but huge thrones to his left and right. As the Elders came into sight, the trio marveled at how they looked pretty much like any other Sinteverete warlock, only with grander, far more elegant robes and decorative jewelry of jade, rubies and onyx. They ranged in age from gray and old to what looked like a fifteen-year-old with piercing vacant eyes—who amazingly sat on the lead Elder's throne. Vasser couldn't hide his surprise. He, like Layluna and Maysiff, had never laid eyes on an Elder, much less seen one so young. Almost no one in either clan chose a form so young because it reminded everyone of what they were missing and would never have again. The audacity of this Elder was like a slap in the face to all three of them.

After a moment, the stone turntable ground to a stop, and they were all face-to-face. A very tense air vibrated between them with excited molecules, and it was Vasser who finally broke the silence, "Say it."

"It is true," the lead Elder said flatly. "All your wild inner speculations are indeed fact. You, them," motioning his head towards Layluna and Maysiff, "you will all be eliminated. First, we will enjoy gambling and games of chance on the outcome of the war before we ultimately replace every Sinteverete and every Pentavi with a new breed. Every. Last. One. Of. You."

"Replace...?" Vasser continued.

"Yes, with a more malleable breed of Sinteverete Nevuscar soldier, much like yourself, only without any soul - without any possibility for a situation exactly like this," the Lead Elder sneered.

Nodding, Vasser went on, "And immortality for the seven of you."

"Correct; however, we have perfected the Nevuscar magic through our Pentavi experimentation. Not only have we discovered a way to conjure ourselves into Nevuscar, we have found a way to heal without the formation of scar tissue. We will forever remain as we are - pristine, powerful...*perfect*." The Lead Elder held his evil smirk. "That said, we like our army of Nevuscar warriors with their scars. It illustrates experience, endurance and encourages fear. More importantly, it indicates their position beneath us."

"And the Pentavi?" Vasser asked before Layluna could.

Speaking to Vasser's question, the Lead Elder replied, "We have no need for lower males *or* females; they will all be eliminated entirely."

Layluna joined the conversation with a pointed tone, "How were you able to capture so many Pentavi women for experimentation?"

The lead Elder never took his eyes off Vasser, "You can tell your uppity concubine that our vast supply of Pentavi volunteers were provided graciously by their own Elders."

Layluna, Maysiff and even Vasser gasped in unison.

Inconceivably, seven slots suddenly opened up in the floor behind the three truth seekers. Seven elaborately decorated thrones that Layluna and Maysiff recognized immediately rose up out of the openings, their backs to them. They, too, were on a large, round stone that began to turn and face them. To Layluna and Maysiff it seemed like an eternity, but eventually, there they were, the seven Pentavi Elder women staring them in the eyes.

Layluna nodded slowly, furious, "Thank you. Thank you for confirming everything for me. Thank you for proving I was right to suspect you. Thank you for outing yourselves as spineless, greedy conformists. And finally, and most importantly, thank you for saving us the journey back to collect your heads."

"Silence, Layluna." The lead Pentavi Elder, a platinum-haired, gorgeous older stately woman, spoke out. She held up her hand reassuringly, "We don't expect you to understand this..."

"Oh, I understand it just fine," Layluna said calmly.

"Absolutely, you pious, poisonous political patsies," Maysiff hissed.

It was Layluna's turn to hold her hand up reassuringly to Maysiff, who bottled the anger for now, but was ready to pop her top at the first word.

The lead Pentavi Elder spoke calmly, almost soothingly, "We understand your anger and bewilderment. There was just no other way, Layluna. The Sinteverete were getting too strong with their dark magic, poisoning the land, the animals, and they were threatening us with their presence every moment of every day. We had to arrive at an arrangement, and this is it. For all its failings, for all its sacrifices, it is the most logical, pragmatic solution to the millions and millions of years we have been at war."

"Bitch, you can stop right there. I noticed your grand future plans only include yourselves. Typical. How could you? How could you sell out all the Pentavi women? Their blood is on your hands," Layluna screamed in her anger.

"We, the Elders—the first—will serve as the undiluted, pristine embodiment of the Pentavi gender. There will only ever need to be the Seven of us, and the Seven Sinteverete Nevuscar Elders, and our army. Together, unified, we will take the Earth realm—all the realms. We will divide them between us and shape them to our needs. Reclon, the other war realms will be cleared of their inhabitants and made available to us. We will finally live in peace," the Pentavi Lead Elder spoke eloquently, folding her hands into her lap.

"Pristine; there's that word again, only out of your lips instead of the Sinteverete Elders. Fucking oligarchy, it was there in front of us the entire time." Layluna tensed, arriving at a decision. "Still, the only crime is not learning the lesson." Layluna struck.

She was upon her lead Elder quicker than summer lightning and beheaded her with Beauty. She already had a hand in her hair and pulled her severed head from her shoulders, forever frozen in a rictus of shock. She then attached the grizzly trophy to her hip using the Ceridome wraps.

Maysiff roared and leapt at the Pentavi Elders, transforming into full yaggowar. She dragged the first one she could get her claws into out of her precious throne and ate her heart straight from her chest.

The lead Sinteverete elder began laughing devilishly while clapping his hands. "Now, this is a show."

Vasser used the distraction to whisper chant a subtle spell that stole the mouths from four of the seven Sinteverete Elders. They clawed frantically at their faces as the young one, along with the other two Elders, levitated up off their thrones and began to whisper chant, but Vasser had plans for them too. He opened a massive portal behind them, and all of Reclons hellish creatures came pouring out, the ones that could fit anyway, and flooded the chamber with all varieties of abominations. The Elders, far from war hearty, shrieked and cowered. Only the young one showed no fear. He waved his hand while continuing to chant, and the other four Elders suddenly had their mouths again, while many of the Reclon freaks exploded into salt. Vasser quickly had Sepultura out and at the boy's throat, stifling his chants. "Shut your selfish mouth, or I'll give you one to chant through in your neck."

Without warning, the Wrecking Ball reached up and grabbed Vasser by his floating leg. He swung him unceremoniously around and through a stone pillar that disintegrated in a hail of rock and rubble. "Respect your Elders, upstart."

Vasser shook off the attack and stood immediately. "Where's your playmate?"

"Right here, honeysuckle." Bael sang, emerging from the darkness, looking almost as bad as the Wrecking Ball now. "You didn't think you were going to get away, did you? It'll take more than a mountain to put me out to pasture, old boy. Got a few more skin stories thanks to you, though. Figures I'd get demoted on the day of my promotion, but I'm not going to let it spoil this victory for me." Vasser had one eye on Bael and another on the Sinteverete Elders, who were already casting portals to escape.

"You fucking cowards," Vasser screamed while stealing a look over to Layluna and Maysiff, who had already massacred three of their Elders. Layluna already had two heads on her hip and was working on sawing off the third one that Maysiff had mauled. Unfortunately, the other four had already escaped through portals, leaving Layluna and Maysiff to rejoin the fight with Vasser and the two scabs.

As the head Sinteverete Elder child began to duck through the portal, Vasser called out to him, "What's your name?"

The sneering youth called back, "Master," before making good his escape. Vasser bellowed in anger with Bael and the Wrecking Ball hanging off of each arm like chains. Vasser began to chant, but it was no whisper. Maysiff, still a yaggowar, tackled the Wrecking Ball, and Layluna plowed Beauty through Bael's right arm, pinning it to his chest and forcing him back several yards. Vasser's final words filled the chamber with an ear-splitting echo. The words made Bael explode into a thousand pieces of bone, rib, loin and shank. Layluna bathed blissfully in the blood baptism and licked her fingers greedily. Instantly, Vasser puked up a few pounds of salt but then quickly turned his fury towards the Wrecking Ball, still duking it out with Maysiff.

He levitated earnestly over to their position and snatched up the human wound by the scruff of his scarred neck and reeled him up into the air like a mischievous puppy.

Maysiff wasn't about to let him go without her pound of flesh and savagely bit off his right leg, swallowing it whole without mercy. Several of Reclons monstrosities scurried around the edge of the fight, grabbing scraps of Bael and whatever else they could find to eat. After a moment, the beasts that had eaten pieces of Bael began to vomit violently and purged the cursed flesh. The scraps began coming together sickeningly as Bael tried to reconstitute himself. Maysiff looked at Layluna worried but then only let out a massive burp. She shrugged her shoulders.

Layluna called to her, "I guess the Wrecking Ball agrees with you."

The Wrecking Ball wrapped his ropy hands around the back of Vasser's head and mouth, keeping him from whisper chanting, but Vasser used his other hand to reach slowly into the Nevuscar's chest and pull out his heart. The Wrecking Ball went from choking Vasser's face to both hands over the sealing hole in his chest. Vasser dropped the meaty man like a sack of shit while holding onto his still beating heart. Vasser began chanting and turned the Wrecking Ball's heart into a roaring fireball. The Wrecking Ball consequently burst into flame as well and began screaming like an animal caught in a snare. He ran around recklessly, scattering the bewildered atrocities that continued to pour in through the portal to Reclon Vasser had opened.

A massive, monstrous hand with squirming maggot parasites the size of pythons writhing around in its skin suddenly reached in through the Reclon portal, filling it. It grasped around wildly at any-thing that moved with its horny, boil-covered hand and finally found Maysiff. It grabbed hold, strangling the yaggowar right out of her. She instantly transformed back into herself under the crushing strength of the Reclon titan. Vasser and Layluna rushed to free her and tried to pry the clawed fingers apart but could not move them an inch.

The Wrecking Ball, still engulfed in flames, managed to wrestle hold of a Reclon beast and tore it viciously in half. He used its blood to extinguish the flames on his flesh.

He now stood there, smoldering and smoking like a leg of lamb on a spit. He reached inside the mangled beast and grabbed hold of a long, large, thick femur before tearing it free. He snapped it sickly with his bare hands and jabbed the sharp end into his leg stump. Scar tissue began wrapping itself around the bone, giving him an absurd prosthetic with a set of bony condyles to hobble around on. He began scrapping piles of Bael together to try and hasten his merger while Vasser and Layluna fought fiercely to save Maysiff.

A sinewy, ropy form began to emerge out of Bael's gut pile, so the trio had precious little time. Vasser chanted and closed off the portal, severing the huge appendage and dropping it sickly to the floor like a million pounds of rotten meat. Other Reclon freaks quickly began to feast on it as it convulsed before finally releasing Maysiff. She instantly drew in a tattered breath and began bleeding from her mouth. Layluna rushed to her side immediately as Vasser bum-rushed the Wrecking Ball and chopped off his head with Sepultura. He kicked it like a soccer ball and sent it skittering away. Bael, now a spindly, skinless horrorshow, grabbed Vasser's mouth from behind, allowing the Wrecking Ball to search for his head.

Maysiff was in bad shape, her bones crushed and her insides in ruin. Layluna cried and screamed at the same time, but Maysiff managed to speak, "I'll be fine, go...go help Vasser. NOW!" She coughed up pulpy, fresh rivulets of blood, rooting Layluna to the spot in indecision. "Goooo," Maysiff demanded, so Layluna howled in agony, transformed into her massive saber-toothed yagowarr form, and swiftly galloped off to help Vasser.

She swatted the Wrecking Ball's head away like a cat toy at the same moment he laid his hands on it. In an instant, she was upon Bael and clamped her jaws around his unnatural body, tearing him free of Vasser and tossing him explosively through several stone columns. The elaborate stone ceiling above suddenly groaned like an old man about to collapse as several other weight-bearing columns cracked and crumbled. The ceiling had massive fractures now snaking through it and threatened to come down at any moment. Vasser threw a spell at Bael, but he blocked it with his still-forming right arm.

Bael used the opportunity to conjure a dark rune that began spinning, resembling a giant twirling circular saw blade, and sent it pinwheeling dangerously at Maysiff's neck. He was hoping to take out the injured warrior and even the odds.

Layluna transformed into herself in an instant and threw Beauty end-over-end into the path of the deadly rune. It stabbed into the stone floor with a loud thunk, right as the rune arrived to decapitate Maysiff. Beauty shattered the spell into a thousand embers, but the blade itself shattered as well, leaving only the handle falling uselessly to the floor.

Bale's grizzly head and neck now had enough flesh and cartilage to croak out words, so he spoke, "That's ancient Sinteverete magic, you fucking slut. I found the spell after spotting your blade last time we danced."

Layluna screamed and projected a hundred Ceridome wraps with razor-sharp ends directly at the walking nightmare, very close to being whole again. Bael conjured a portal underneath his feet and disappeared as the wraps snapped like a whip over his head. Without warning, he reappeared behind her, entirely scared but whole again. He still had his dick, at least, she thought. Well, sort of. He went to grab her, but she leapt high into the air with amazing speed and dexterity before coming down hard in a superhero pose.

Vasser was on Bael in an instant from above, cutting him in half vertically with Sepultura. It was such a clean cut, Bael hardly noticed, coming back together seamlessly. He kicked out hard and connected with Vasser's balls, crumpling him to the ground. In a flash, Bael had his arms around Vasser's neck, cutting off his air supply and his words.

Layluna saw the Wrecking Ball reattach his angry head, so she ran back over to Maysiff to protect her. Maysiff was going in and out of consciousness at this point, and Layluna didn't know how much longer she could hold on.

"Couple petals for the plucking," Wrecking Ball promised.

"Come and get it, fatso," Layluna beckoned.

"Hey, I'm just big-boned," he joked before charging her at full speed.

Layluna felt naked fighting without Beauty but began twirling herself around and using her Ceridome wraps to transform herself into a giant, whirling death machine, with hundreds of spinning, razor-sharp straps flying around. The Wrecking Ball amazingly charged directly at her, the wraps shredding his rocky flesh to ribbons, but he hardly seemed to notice.

He grabbed her around the waist with his massive mits and squeezed the fight right out of her. She withered within his crushing hands that encapsulated her like wet concrete. She beat on his hands as he used his much larger size to force her head into his yawning mouth, boasting a set of perfectly straight, beautiful teeth. Layluna inwardly snickered while trying to keep his maw jacked apart with her trembling arms. He had her in up to her chest now and began to bring his beautiful teeth together around her like a steel bear trap. His monstrous canines and molars were now cutting deeply into her flesh as she fought futilely. Thinking fast, she exhaled her Alma entirely and transformed inside his jaws, forcing them explosively apart. The top half of his head snapped back like a flip top, and he released her. She was triple his size now and flopped on top of him like a kitty on a cracker. She began playing with him as a cat plays with mice, swatting him around and playfully biting him. The Nevuscar frantically tried to bring his head back together for the second time that battle.

Vasser continued to struggle with Bael, in a deadlock. He couldn't chant, but Bael couldn't conjure, so it became a match of strength.

Vasser forced Bael's arms apart with his bare hands, then got down and dirty and bit the Nevuscar warrior's arm until he let go. Without warning, Bael transported to where Maysiff was, grabbed up a massive rock and threatened to coup de gras her with it. Before he could smash her defenseless head, Layluna swatted him with her gigantic paw and sent him flying through more weakened pillars.

The ceiling finally collapsed and rained a hundred feet of the crumbling tower down on their war-torn heads. Vasser managed to cast a protective sphere around Layluna and Maysiff, but was buried in the devastation along with Bael and the Wrecking Ball. Layluna transformed back to herself, allowing the sphere to shrink and spare Vasser the energy. She watched wide-eyed as a tonnage of rock buried them in their protective sphere. She turned her attention back to Maysiff, who was struggling to pull air.

"Hold on, my love. Just a bit longer. Vasser will fix you up, I promise. He'll make you take a honey, lavender bath, though," she said, hoping to make Maysiff chuckle, but there was no response. "Fight, dammit, fight," Layluna screamed desperately and wild-eyed with fear.

Maysiff fought back to consciousness and looked Layluna in the eye, determined, "I can cut it..," she said, gasping, "I can cut it, my...love." She shook and shuddered but held on like a warrior. The power sphere began to close in tightly around them, threatening their position. The edge was right against Layluna's shoulder and head.

"That's right, baby. We can cut it. We can cut it," Layluna lied and cried.

Suddenly there was a familiar face pressed grotesquely against the failing protective sphere like a kid at a candy store—it was the Wrecking Ball. He forced his huge, reaching and rancorous hands through the rubble and greedily clawed at Maysiff. She weakly cried as he closed them around her head and proceeded to drag her towards his yawning mouth.

"This will be just as sweet as pie..." he promised as his mouth opened impossibly again to accommodate her. Layluna fought heroically with every last atom of her strength to hold onto her true love, but she had no leverage in the collapsing protection shield, and Maysiff went head-first inside the Wrecking Ball's hungry gob.

"NOOOOOOOOOOOOOOOOO," Layluna cry screamed as she watched Maysiff disappear entirely into his open mouth. He closed his wrinkled, deformed and coiled lips around her big toe and used his finger to force it inside like a fat kid with the last morsel of food. He then began chewing slowly, savoring every loud crunch of bone.

Layluna gritted her teeth and let out a guttural growl that shook the heavens. Her Alma began to smoke out from between her clenched and growing teeth. As she transformed into the hulking yaggowar, she forced the sphere and rubble to expand outward.

As Layluna grew, so did the protective sphere. The Wrecking Ball suddenly realized he was sharing a protective sphere with the angriest, meanest, largest yaggowar the realms had ever seen. His gloating smile faltered. Layluna pressed her massive, moist yaggowar nose against his, growling thunderously.

"You ain't mad, are ya?" The Wrecking Ball asked sheepishly.

She parted her megalodon sized teeth ever so slowly, growling fiercely the entire time. Her saliva drenched the Wrecking Ball's face as her eager tongue lolled out and invited him inside. He looked fretfully into her huge cat eyes and saw his own fear reflected back at him. She slowly leaned in and engulfed him as he begged her not to eat him. "I'm all gristle," he pleaded. "I won't die in your belly. I'll forever give you indigestion beating on the sides of your stomach." His pleas fell on deaf ears, though, and she pulled him further inside using her tusks.

Finally, she slammed her jaws shut around him, cutting the miserable mage in half at his waist. He cried out pitifully like a whining coyote, and she quickly popped his head like a grape between her monstrous molars. It was her turn now to chew slowly and savor every bite. She ground him to pulp inside her watering mouth and slurped up his twitching legs like noodles. Within seconds, she had every bit of him in her stomach.

The cracking and dwindling sphere finally gave up the ghost and faltered out. Layluna was left using her yaggowar size and strength to continue expanding the debris outward; every second, she thought her strength would give out and her breath would leave her. The boulders threatened to close in around her, sealing her doom. Then she thought of Maysiff and detonated like a nuclear bomb; exploding out of the suffocating stone, she was cut, battered, and bleeding, but with a full stomach. She quickly began to sniff the rubble fervently, looking for Vasser. She located his scent and began pawing through the rock to free him. After what seemed like forever, she found him and pulled him out, using her teeth like a lion would with her cub. She laid him down softly and licked the length of his body with her enormous tongue.

After a while, she transformed back into herself, clutching her turning stomach. She knew she wouldn't be able to keep her meal down for long, but figured it'd be long enough. She shook Vasser and begged him to wake up. Amazingly, his eye's fluttered, and they snapped open. He was quick to find his feet, Blade of Black in hand. "Where is Maysiff? Is she alright?" Layluna crumpled to the ground and began sobbing.

"No." Absolute shock etched itself across his face. "No, she has to be alright. Where? What? NOOOOOOOOOOOOO," He yelled so loudly it scattered boulders the size of a full-grown bock like crumpled paper. "WHO. DID. IT?" He demanded.

With that, Layluna fully transformed back into a yaggowar and puked up what was left of the Wrecking Ball. Vasser walked over to the pulsating mass of muscle and viscera and spat on it. Layluna transformed back into herself, wrecked with loss, and clenched her fists and teeth while staring holes through the quivering mass of scar tissue. "This dickless piece of shit ate her, so I ate him." She shouted and cried all at the same time.

"I vow he will spend eternity paying this debt. I will make it my life's mission to ensure he spends every second of every day in agonizing pain. You hear me in there, meatball? I'm going to get creative and craft a cage worthy of your malignant nature. He began to whisper chant and pulled all the foul pieces of the freshly ground Wrecking Ball together into a perfect sphere of roiling, toiling protein. He compressed the sphere into a small ball that fit nicely between his first finger and thumb. Afterwhich, he levitated it up above his open hand and conjured a black chain around it. Placing the chain around his neck, he held up the swirling, glossy meat colored ball and gazed at it with sour hatred. "Live well, old friend."

Layluna slowly walked to his side and looked at the necklace, "Is he suffering in there?"

"More than you can possibly imagine," Vasser growled.

"Good," she said tonelessly.

Vasser suddenly doubled over and began throwing up salt for what seemed like forever. It was impossible the amount he purged, after which he looked positively embattled. "Are you going to be alright?" she asked him in a deeply wounded voice.

"I'm so sorry, Layluna." He bowed his head in absolute anguish. "She was your true mate, and I know what it's like to lose someone like that. The pain is immeasurable. I...I had such great affection for Maysiff, and I will spend my eternal life by your side, remembering her, and seeking retribution for as long as you live. I am forever in your service. We will find our hard-earned heads from today's battle and make trophies of them." The words actually smoked as they left his poisonous lips. "We will stop at nothing to guarantee the remaining Elders join them—from the neck up." Vasser's eyes became black as a skink's eyes, and he raised a clenched fist towards the sky. "You hear me talking? We are coming for you. No matter the cost, no matter the sacrifice, we will make you answer for everything you have done. All the pain and misery you heaped at the feet of our clans, will be visited upon you a thousandfold."

Layluna hugged him tightly. "Please. Don't let them steal your kindness," She closed her eyes and wept for the first time in hundreds of thousands of years. "Don't let them poison your nobility or rob you of everything that makes you different—better—than they are. Everything that Maysiff held precious about you, everything we both held precious. We noticed the way you stop and smell flowers or the way you watch sunsets. These qualities must persevere, or they win. Your uniqueness, your half smile, your honey scented skin. All these things that make me...made Maysiff... let you into our hearts. We will have our satisfaction, no matter how long it takes, but we will not sacrifice anything else."

Vasser dissolved his tension and held Layluna like she might float away. He cried with her, their tears washing away the uncertainty and pain for a moment. "I will see you under the snow-covered thornwillow trees in winter."

"How's that?" Layluna asked, wiping the tears from her eyes and smiling warmly up to him.

He caught himself and smiled back, "Oh, nothing. It's something I used to say..." Swallowing hard, "It's something I used to say to Zzoveigh. No matter what happened, we would always meet under the snow-covered thornwillow trees in winter." After a long, lingering moment, he added, "I've never missed a winter under those thornwillow trees."

"And you never will," Layluna promised, looking deeply into his eyes. "We are partners in grief, war, and pain, but we are partners. We are bonded."

"We are bonded," Vasser repeated, then kissed her deeply.

Layluna reciprocated, wrapping her arms around him tightly. After the kiss, she remained in his gaze, "Let's collect our heads and finish this. Then we can spend the rest of our time in the realms together, remembering our loved ones."

"Indeed. Maysiff is among them, Layluna." Vasser's eyes showed the truth he spoke.

"As are you, Vasser," she whispered to him. They held each other sweetly for a long time.

Eventually, Layluna let Vasser go and began pawing through the rubble. After a moment, she produced her lead Elder's head, "One down, two more to go."

"Eleven more to go," Vasser corrected as he kneeled down to help her look through the rubble. Vasser stopped abruptly, finding something in the wreckage. "What have we here..."

"What is it?" she asked, looking hard.

Vasser held up Beauty's handle, "It appears Beauty needs a blade."

"Can you help with that," Layluna pressed.

"I'll try," Vasser promised.

"Good enough." She took the handle from him and stared at it. "We will make them pay, Maysiff, and we will not lose ourselves along the way."

Vasser held up the three Elder's heads high, put his arm around Lay-luna, and formed an energy sphere around them. He transported the two of them and their cargo from the ruined top of the Sinteverete tower to a far-off ridgeline close to the poisoned, dying woods. With a whisper, Vasser brought the remaining Sinteverete temple crashing down like it was made of paper.

"A new day today," he said.

"A new day indeed," she agreed, studying his face. "After all that, you still only have the one scar?"

"Just the one," he said humbly.

"Are you ever going to tell me how you got it?" she asked, intrigued.

"One day," he teased.

"I hope you never get another one because of me," Layluna added, kissing his scar.

Vasser smiled, "My dear, I would gladly take on a thousand scars for you."

EPILOGUE

Several Moons Later...

Vasser whispered lightly to himself and opened a door into a gigantic slab of Pentavi granite close to their lands. "See, I knew you could do it," Layluna said excitedly.

"I'm amazed I remember the words," Vasser spoke excitedly.

"So...you think you can fix Beauty?"

"I believe so," he said, trying to sound confident.

"Excellent." Layluna threw her arms around him and kissed him deeply. "So, this is to be our trophy case?"

"It is," Vasser said proudly. He placed the three Elders' heads within the Pentavi granite and whispered it closed. The seams forming the door sealed, but a single, simple rune etched itself into the rock, marking it. "Eleven more to go."

"About that. There, uh, might be one small complication with our vendetta," Layluna ventured.

"Really, what's that? I have the—"

"I'm pregnant." Layluna blurted out.

Vasser looked like a bock caught in tharn. "How can you know? The contraception spell..."

"Trust me, a lady knows." Then she thought for a moment, "Also, I think the contraception spell is somehow tied to Copunocture, but when we started...making love, it...broke the spell."

"I'm going to be a father?" Vasser gasped, the entirety of the situation dawning on him.

"Looks that way, daddy," Layluna smiled and looked up into his astonished eyes.

"I've never been happier in my entire life," Vasser yelled, coming to life. "This is...a big change. Fuck, we can't go off collecting the heads of our Elders now. What are we going to do?"

"Well, the way I see it—all bets are off. We have a child to think about now. It flips our path on its head," Layluna paced back and forth. "While I can't stand the thought of my sisters fighting and dying in Reclon, or the Elders getting away with their genocide, we have to redraw our destiny."

"What are you suggesting?" Vasser asked pleadingly.

"We can hide out in the Mandala realm. Time passes six times slower there than it does here or in the Reclon realm. We can train her, educate her, armor her against our oppressors. Then, we can fight by her side."

"Her?" Vasser asked.

Layluna smiled, "Her."

"How can you know?" Vasser demanded.

"I can sense her Alma. What do you think of Mina as a name?" she asked tentatively.

Vasser sat down hard on a rock and put his head in his hands, "I think it's a beautiful name."

"Mina was Maysiff's favorite name." Layluna hugged Vasser, "Don't worry papa, you'll do great."

"I think this is the most terrified I've ever been in my life," he chuckled.

"Good," Layluna said smiling. "That means you will do it right."

***

"Were you able to find it?" Vasser asked impatiently. "I feel very exposed here." Vasser and Layluna were sifting through the charred remnants of the Typress falls. The sublime beauty lay in ruins, the geo-warmed pools now muddy with silt, and the majestic falls were nothing but water running through the rubble.

Layluna was shoulder deep in the muddy pools, searching around blindly with her hands. "This is such a tragedy. Typress was once so beautiful; now look at it."

"It will heal given time. The war is in Reclon now, so nature will rebuild. What is it exactly that you are looking for?" He wondered what could be so important to risk their lives.

"This," Layluna proclaimed and brought up the fluorescent blue worry stone triumphantly.

"You had me out here in Pentavi land, with a war on and both our Elders hunting for us, to find a stone hidden among a million other stones?" Vasser was exasperated.

"Well, I found it didn't I?" Layluna said, smiling.

"Yes, you did. I'm learning never to doubt you." Vasser couldn't help but smile at his love.

"Learn faster," Layluna demanded.

Vasser huffed melodramatically and conjured a chain for her worry stone. "There, now Maysiff will be with us forever."

Layluna pulled it over her head and kept it next to her heart," Forever," she repeated.

***

Vasser and Layluna stood tensely on the edge of a swirling black portal to the Mandala realm. "This is it," Vasser told Layluna, his arm around her and holding her tightly. "It's important you know that I will never stop fighting to make sure you and Mina are safe."

"Same," Layluna said poignantly. "I think I love that about you."

"I think I love you," Vasser said nonchalantly.

"I think I love you too," Layluna said, putting her hands on his face and turning him toward her. "I know..."

"I know too." They shared a rare and tender kiss that filled them both with hope and promise. "Don't go hiding the marriage stone just yet," Vasser joked.

Layluna held up the blue worry stone and grinned ear-to-ear, "That's precisely what I intend to do." With that, she leapt through the portal into the Mandala realm.

Vasser called out to her, laughing, "I'll give you a full minute to hide it."

Suddenly her hand reached out of the portal, grabbed him by his collar and yanked him through the portal.

When Vasser emerged on the other side, he was struck by how lovely the realm was; the only issue was everything, and I mean everything, was a different shade of blue. Layluna laughed, "Good luck."

Vasser grinned and began to whisper chant, but Layluna silenced him with a kiss, "No cheating, suitor."

Vasser let out a great sigh and began searching, "I don't get one hint?"

"It's within a hundred feet radius," she laughed.

Vasser stiffened, turned and wrapped his arms around her. As he kissed her passionately, he reached inside her wraps and touched the worry stone. "I knew you would never take this off."

"Then you know me." It was Layluna's turn to kiss Vasser passionately.

"And you me." They held each other and watched the blue dwarf sun set behind the myriad shades of blue that comprised the landscape.

***

Eighteen years passed in Val Tebrae and Reclon, where a hundred and eight had passed in the Mandala realm. The war raged on in Reclon between the clans, while in Mandala, Mina had become a fierce warrior, blessed with the advantage of both Pentavi and Sinteverete training. Choosing to remain a gorgeous thirty years of age, Mina flourished and shared a loving, wonderful and fulfilling life there with her parents. However, always looming was the reality that they might be discovered, or at the very least, they would soon have to face the Elders again and try to put an end to the war.

Vasser and Layluna cast the Eonian over Mina on her third birthday and informed her of their complicated plans on her eighteenth. Layluna had Vasser repair Beauty and handed her down to Mina shortly after. Mina took to Beauty like a lion to the trees and mastered her in no time at all. Beauty's new blade still had the fatter, half spear-tipped end and narrow neck carved from white Pentavi granite, with serrations on the top side and new bleeder symbols carved into the surface. Beauty retained her original handle, which fit into Mina's grasp like a lover's hand. Layluna was a proud, loving mother who beamed with pride every time Mina walked into view. She taught her absolutely everything she knew, and Mina was like a thirsty sponge absorbing every detail.

Vasser was also a wonderful, patient, and kind father. He loved Mina more than anything in the realms, and it showed. He would spend hours upon hours training her, educating her, and teaching her about the Sinteverete—good and bad.

Mina couldn't ask for more attentive, dedicated and loving parents. She flourished there with them until one summer day...

***

Mina was in the garden with Layluna, toiling in the surprising heat of the neighboring dwarf sun, when a snowflake lazily landed on her nose. "What's this? A snowflake in summer?" Mina proclaimed. Then it hit her like a bolt from the blue. "Nevuscar," she screamed. Layluna snapped her attention towards the sky, and there, swirling above them, was the growing Nevuscar portal. Snow began pouring out of the massive black hole, freezing their crops, as well as their hearts.

"Well, well, well, there's my favorite pussycat," a familiar voice called out from between the blue corn. Bael, Vasser's former second in command of the Nevuscar – now last in command – emerged from the center row, naked and covered in thick, corded scars like The Wrecking Ball, with a coarse coppery mohawk growing through the asphalt of his head as best it could. The only thing he was wearing was what looked like a sleek, maroon plate of etched armor around the back of his head that covered his ears. His filthy presence wilted the crop of corn with his toxic aura. "And look here. A Yasmani Ro." He began to wag his finger at Layluna, scolding her. "That's a no no."

Layluna rose up slowly from her aqua-colored radishes, and she may as well have had a storm cloud over her head. "Bael."

"In the flesh," He proclaimed.

"So to speak," Layluna corrected him. "I see my husband left you as handsome on the outside as you are on the inside."

Six Nevuscar warriors suddenly emerged from the remaining six rows of corn. Layluna recognized four of them, but the other two, completely void of scars, were unknown to her.

"I see you've replenished your ranks with a new breed." Layluna colloquially said, vying for any intel she could coax out of them.

One of the two new, unblemished Nevuscar fighters stepped forward in front of Bael. "You are correct. I am Mayax the Malevolent. I am the leader of the Nevuscar." Mayax was disarmingly handsome. His long, flowing black hair framed a gaunt, angular face before joining his long, burly braided beard down below. However, instead of an Absence of Light cloak, he wore a sleek, intimidatingly wicked black helmet. The other Nevuscar, including Beal, were also wearing helmets, although theirs were maroon. Mayax wore no cape or cloak, but he wore thorny, form-fitting armor carved from the impenetrable shell of a Reclon titan. The other five Nevuscar boasted similar armor instead of the traditional leathers that Vasser still wore. Bael, once second in command, now last, wore nothing but the helmet, another similarity to the Wrecking Ball.

Layluna was without her Ceridome wraps or any weapons for that matter. All she had was a spade, which she clutched as though it were a sword.

Mina tore off her dirty burlap poncho to reveal she was wearing Layluna's Ceridome wraps, and sheathed within them, as always, was Beauty. Mina pulled her out, showing off the new blade.

"Your daughter is beautiful," Mayax admitted flatly.

"Beauty is a blade," Mina replied stoically.

Layluna chuckled in spite of herself.

"Indeed. What is your name?" Mayax inquired casually.

Mina, trying to stall for time, "I am Mina, and I guess you are the unnatural abomination conjured without a womb by your Elders?"

"I am, but there is no need to try and stall us," Mayax said, "Vasser has arrived."

Vasser walked briskly from behind Layluna and Mina, with Sepultura out and at the ready. "Took you guys long enough to find us."

"We found you; that's all that matters," Mayax stated coldly.

Vasser began to whisper chant, but Mayax smiled and tapped the side of his helmet. "New toys for a new breed." Vasser immediately charged Mayax with the tip of Sepultura leading the way, but Mayax didn't flinch an inch. Vasser suddenly froze in mid-charge, Sepultura millimeters from Mayax's eye. "We have accomplished much in the last eighteen years," Mayax taunted. He reached into Vasser's leathers, fished out the swirling round pendant that contained the Wrecking Ball, and yanked it off his neck.

Vassser spoke through clenched teeth, "We will meet again, Mayax."

"Promises, promises," Mayax said cooly. With a blink of his eye, Mayax turned Vasser into a pillar of salt. Layluna wailed out mournfully, clutching the worry stone around her neck before joining him in a twin pillar of salt.

"NOOOO," Mina screamed, but she knew better than to charge the Nevuscar leader or his cronies. "Undo it." She demanded threateningly.

Mayax maintained his smug smile and shook his head. "What will you do, little girl? What can you possibly do? This is not a circumstance that facilitates your calling for demands."

Mayax nodded and motioned to the other six Nevuscar. They put their hands together, almost as if to pray, and a gargantuan slab of Pentavi granite levitated above the corn and over to their position. The tall monolith slowly touched down, crushing the squash and pumpkins in their garden.

Mina looked on, confused and frantic, "What the Hell are you going to do with that?"

Mayax simply ignored her, looked to the slab of Pentavi granite, and a large door opened up in it. He turned his head towards the two pillars of salt that were Mina's loving parents not two minutes before and levitated them inside the granite with his mind.

"Don't do it, mage," Mina promised death and destruction with her eyes. "Don't fucking do it."

Mayax continued to smile pleasantly as the Pentavi granite sealed around her prisoner parents. A strange rune of embracing figures etched itself into the slick surface.

"There, I've done it. What will you do now?" Mayax's smile widened to a toothy grin.

Mina stood there like a statue for a very long time with nothing to say.

"Well?" Mayax asked again, but Mina remained there, motionless. "Looks like Mina has moxy." He strolled up to her and tapped the tip of her nose with his first finger, dispersing her cast-off skin like an ash cloud into the wind. "She's clever, this one. Apparently, they've done some upgrades as well; never seen that little trick. Find her." The other six Nevuscar levitated up into the air and went in six different directions. Mayax chuckled as he attached Vassers Wrecking Ball prison pendant to his belt.

Mina watched them from a far-off ridgeline. "They're still alive; that's all that matters." She then whisper chanted, snapped her fingers, and disappeared.

***

"Hey. You. What the hell are you doing in my garden?"

Mina sprang awake as a strange little old man poked her with a stick. He was wearing strange sandals with tall wooden slats, a round straw hat with a pointed top, and tattered robes that looked like they needed a wash. She couldn't understand a word he had said but tried to speak with him anyway. She used very docile, calm tones to try and communicate to him that she meant no harm, "Mina," she said, tapping her chest.

"I don't give a damn who you are; get the Hell outta my garden," he continued to clamor in a foreign tongue.

Mina shrugged her shoulders and shook her head. The old man sighed a great sigh and motioned for her to follow him inside his home. What choice did either of them have? She followed the tiny little old man, who lived in a gorgeous, intricately carved wooden house with framed paper doors and straw mats. Mysterious runes painted on long paper scrolls hung smartly from the walls inside. She stole a glance over her shoulder back at the garden and marveled at how beautiful it was. There were preciously little trimmed trees in stone pots and lovely flowers everywhere. Large trees with amazing pink blossoms lined the garden's perimeter, and stone statues of strange men stood throughout. There was so much color Mina couldn't believe it. She had spent over a hundred years with only a thousand different shades of blue, so this was a sensory overload. In any case, she reeled in her fascination.

Once inside, the little old man poured her a cup of tea from a delicate teapot while setting his hat down on the table. He poured himself a cup, bowed and drank. She bowed her head as well and drank with him. The tea was absolutely delicious.

She suddenly gulped it down greedily, but the little old man protested with a grunt and lightly smacked her hand. He shook his head no and demonstrated how to sip it slowly and politely. Mina rolled her eyes, which proffered her another smack from the little old man. She relented, smiled and demonstrated she could properly sip tea. To this, he smiled a great big, gummy grin and clapped the table with his hand. He then clapped his chest and said, "Geezer."

"Geezer," Mina repeated carefully.

Geezer shook his head happily up and down while continuing to pat his chest. Mina smiled and thanked him.

***

After tea, Geezer motioned for Mina to follow him outside. A magnificent sunset stole Mina's breath away, and she gawked at it for what seemed like an eternity. She finally snapped out of it and saw Geezer standing there patiently waiting for her to finish taking it all in. When he was certain she was with him again, he led her down a path through the garden and towards a clearing. Once they got there, he selected a strangely simple but beautiful forged sword from a modest armament. He tapped the sheath that contained Beauty within her Ceridome wraps and smiled that silly smile. She looked at him with a wrinkled brow and shrugged her shoulders, "What, you want to fight," she asked, punching the air with her hands.

He quickly shook his head vigorously up and down.

She laughed and condescended down to him, "Wow. Listen, little fella; I'd hate to accidentally injure you playing too rough..." But before she could finish her sentence, he moved like a phantom, had her on her ass, and bent her wrist impossibly backward. "Hey," she protested. He let her go and helped her up with a smile. She brushed herself off and tried to sucker punch the old timer, but he was already ten moves ahead of her. There she was again, staring up at the sky, on her ass. He leaned in over her and helped her back up with that same smile. Geezer grabbed hold of her waist and walked her to the center of the clearing. He motioned for her to stay there and positioned himself in front of her. He bowed to her, and she reciprocated. Geezer raised his sword, let out an impressive battle cry, and charged her. She was out with Beauty now, her old friend giving her the focus she needed. As if moving in slow motion, Mina hooked Geezer's blade in Beauty's hook and snapped it like a twig before putting the salty samurai on his own ass. She leaned over him, extended her hand and helped him up with a smile. Once he was up and stable, he looked at his broken sword and nodded slowly, with his grin widening across his weathered face.

"Sorry about that," Mina apologized, but Geezer waived it off and selected another strange weapon of war. "You know, for a little old guy, you're sure full of piss and vinegar."

To this, he nodded his head again slowly and smiled his silly smile.
***

Later that night, Mina lay on a straw mat in Geezer's main living space and cried for her parents. She was quiet about it, but Geezer could see her through a gap in the wall. He knew she had sustained a great loss and was a stranger out of place.

The next morning, as the sun came up, Mina opened her eyes and saw Geezer staring down at her, smiling. "Whoa," she said, startled. He patted her on the shoulder and led her to the garden. There, he put a little piece of rice paper in her hand. She unfolded it and saw a simple but beautiful brush drawing of a young girl. Geezer patted the drawing and then patted his heart. He then pointed over to a gravestone in the center of the garden. He grabbed her hands in his and pulled her down to a kneeling position so they could be face-to-face. He patted her heart, then he patted his own heart again and hugged her. Unable to contain it, Mina let loose her floodgates of sorrow and burst into tears while Geezer held her tight and patted her back. He shushed her and stroked her hair while she let it all out.

When Mina had dried her last tear, Geezer let her go. She stood up, and he smiled at her. She smiled back at him. He grabbed her hand and led her back inside to a bowl of rice and a dumpling. He pointed to the bowl of rice and said, "gohan." She didn't repeat it, so he stuck his finger in the rice and said, "gohan."

"Oh, rice. Rice is gohan." She clapped.

He nodded his head, pleased with her. Then he tapped the bowel and said, "Cho."

This time she repeated, "Cho. Bowel is cho."

He nodded his head again and gave a reassuring grunt. Then he tapped himself, to which she replied, "Geezer."

He nodded and smiled again. She really liked this guy.

The End

About the author

Justin lives in North Carolina with his beautiful wife and lovely step-daughter. He works as a CT tech during the day, but his true love is art. He is an artist and writer at heart. He enjoys bringing his characters to life and challenging his writing skills by changing genres. His beautiful wife is the one who got him into romance. He loves living in the mountains and hiking but has lived all over the country and enjoys writing about all of these various locations.

You can find out more about him and his stories on his website.

https://www.justinbourneboring.com

ALSO BY

A Thousand Scars for You series:

Beauty is a Blade (Book 1)
https://books2read.com/BeautyisaBlade
Violence & Roses (Book 2)
https://books2read.com/ViolenceRoses
A Hell of No Hearts (Book 3)
https://books2read.com/HellofnoHearts

Standalone Contemporary Romance:

Beau-laid
https://books2read.com/beau-laid